Trapped with the monster . . .

Elizabeth was about to reach out and touch the doll when the figure moved, lifting its head. Two menacing eyes looked up at her.

It's the monster! Elizabeth's heart pounded in her chest as she took a step backward, preparing to flee.

At that exact moment the door she'd so carefully propped open slammed shut with a bang.

Elizabeth backed up against the door. "N-No," she gasped. "Please, don't—"

The monster reached out with large, clawlike hands. The flesh on its face was melting, and as it stepped closer to Elizabeth she saw the monster's eyes were glowing, as if a fire burned within.

"What—what do you want?" Elizabeth stammered.

The monster didn't answer. Instead it reached out, its arms oozing, and wrapped its claw fingers around Elizabeth's neck!

"No!" she screamed, gasping for air.

SWEET VALLEY TWINS

The Beast Must Die

Written by
Jamie Suzanne

Created by
FRANCINE PASCAL

BANTAM BOOKS
NEW YORK·TORONTO·LONDON·SYDNEY·AUCKLAND

To Katherine Beatrice Powell Prescott

RL 4, 008-012

THE BEAST MUST DIE

A Bantam Book / September 1996

*Sweet Valley High® and Sweet Valley Twins® are
registered trademarks of Francine Pascal*

Conceived by Francine Pascal

*Produced by Daniel Weiss Associates, Inc.
33 West 17th Street
New York, NY 10011*

Cover art by James Mathewuse

ISBN: 0-553-48204-1

Published simultaneously in the United States and Canada

*Bantam Books are published by Bantam Books, a division of Bantam
Doubleday Dell Publishing Group, Inc. Its trademark, consisting of the
words "Bantam Books" and the portrayal of a rooster, is Registered in the
U.S. Patent and Trademark Office and in other countries. Marca
Registrada. Bantam Books, 1540 Broadway, New York, New York 10036.*

PRINTED IN THE UNITED STATES OF AMERICA

OPM   0 9 8 7 6 5 4 3 2 1

One

"Elizabeth, we're going to die in here!" Jessica Wakefield shouted to her sister. She pounded on the heavy wooden door, which had somehow locked shut behind them. "Please! Wake up! Someone! Anyone! Let us out of here!" she cried desperately.

Elizabeth stared at her twin sister, her heart pounding in her chest. She didn't even know how they'd gotten into this horrible situation, but they were trapped in a secret bedroom on the third floor of the Riccoli mansion—there was no way out! And from the strong smell of smoke that was seeping through the floorboards, it was obvious that somewhere, somehow, the house had caught on fire!

Downstairs the five Riccoli kids Elizabeth and Jessica were baby-sitting for were in serious danger. *And we can't save them as long as we're trapped up here,* Elizabeth thought, dread rising in her throat.

Frantically she looked at her watch. "Look—it's almost time for Mrs. Riccoli to get home!" she cried, showing Jessica her watch. "When she gets back from SVU—"

"We won't have to worry about dying in here because she'll *kill* us," Jessica moaned. "Can you imagine what she's going to think? When she drives up and sees her house on fire?"

"Well . . . maybe she'll be late," Elizabeth said, her hands trembling as she began pounding on the door.

"But what good would that do? If she doesn't come home on time, we might really be in trouble," Jessica said. "Like, we might not ever get out of here! No one even knows we're upstairs. They might not even know this room *exists*."

"We'll get out," Elizabeth said determinedly. "And it's—it's not that big a fire."

"Elizabeth! How do we even know how big it is?" Jessica argued. "If we can smell smoke, it's bad enough." She shook her head. "Don't you remember *any*thing from our fire safety day at school?"

Elizabeth frowned, looking nervously around the room for something she could use to smash open the door. But it was only an old bedroom that had once belonged to a child. The room had been sealed up for years apparently, though Elizabeth had no idea why. It was filled with stuffed animals, picture books, and dolls—nothing Elizabeth could use as a weapon to break down the door.

"Maybe we could take those big wooden boards

off the windows," she suggested to Jessica, who was still pounding on the locked door.

"And then what?" Jessica asked. "We're on the third floor. We can't exactly jump."

"Maybe we could scale down to the second floor," Elizabeth said.

"With what?" Jessica replied. "A hair ribbon from one of those dolls?" She frowned. "Actually, maybe that's not a bad idea." She picked a doll with curly blond hair off the bed. "Hey, this is kind of pretty. It reminds me of that doll Grandma Wakefield gave me—you know, back in first grade? Do you think my hair would look nice if I curled it like this?"

Elizabeth shook her head. "Jessica, how can you even think about hairstyles right now?"

"Well, excuse me for trying to help!" Jessica put the doll back on the bed. "I guess I'll just start tying some sheets together!"

Elizabeth watched as her sister tried to yank the sheets off the old, unused bed. Actually it didn't really surprise her that Jessica would start talking about hairstyles in the middle of a fire. The twins were identical on the outside: each had long blond hair, blue-green eyes, and a dimple in her left cheek. But Elizabeth sometimes thought Jessica's main interests were a little frivolous—she could spend hours talking about boys and trying on clothes, and her friends in the Unicorn Club, a group of girls who considered themselves the prettiest and most popular in Sweet Valley Middle School, were the same way. Elizabeth liked to have fun with her friends too, but she wasn't easily distracted from her serious interests—her schoolwork or her work on the *Sweet Valley Sixers*, the sixth-grade newspaper.

And at the moment all she could think about was how horrible it felt to be trapped in a secret bedroom. She couldn't count the number of strange things that had happened since she and Jessica started baby-sitting for Mrs. Riccoli. "Jessica . . . do you think this house is evil? Like . . . more than just haunted?" she asked her sister.

"This thing won't budge!" Jessica said, giving up on pulling the sheet off the bed. "I don't know if this house is evil, but there has to be *some* explanation for all the weird scary stuff that keeps happening. First Juliana's bad dreams, then that creepy old gardener Mr. Brangwen died, then I had that awful dream about the monster. . . ."

Elizabeth shuddered, remembering Jessica's nightmare. It was so vivid in her mind, from Jessica's description—it was almost as if she'd had the dream herself. Mr. Brangwen had warned Elizabeth several times never to fall asleep at the Riccolis' house. And when Jessica did fall asleep there, she'd had the worst dream of her entire life. In the dream a scary monster, its face yellow-black and rotting, had come after her, threatening to hurt her. . . . Elizabeth shuddered just remembering the details Jessica had described to her.

It sounded like the same dream one of the Riccoli kids, Juliana, had been having a little while back. Juliana had been so frightened by the nightmare, she hadn't slept for days. And then some of the other kids started having the same dream too—and what was more, Juliana had even ended up with scratches on her back . . . scratches that neither Elizabeth nor Jessica could find a logical explanation for.

There was something very strange about the Riccoli house, that was for sure. All Elizabeth knew was that years ago, a family called the Sullivans had lived there. No one had inhabited it since, until the Riccolis moved in a few weeks back. Mrs. Riccoli had asked the Wakefield twins and their friends to baby-sit on a fairly regular basis. Her husband hadn't been able to move to Sweet Valley yet, and Mrs. Riccoli worked evenings as a professor at Sweet Valley University. She needed help, and Elizabeth had been happy to take the job at first. But now . . .

Who knows if I'll ever baby-sit again? she thought forlornly, her eyes beginning to tear up from the smoke seeping through the floorboards.

"Shouldn't Mrs. Riccoli have a smoke alarm?" Jessica asked, turning around from the door. "Why isn't that going off? Why aren't the neighbors—"

"Jessica—your hands!" Elizabeth exclaimed. She rushed over to her sister. Jessica's knuckles were bleeding, the skin scraped raw. "You have to stop knocking on the door!"

"Well, what else am I supposed to do?" Jessica asked, her voice hoarse from shouting. "Somebody has to hear us! I don't want to *die* up here. And the kids are downstairs and . . ." She gulped. Her lips were clenched tightly together, as if she were trying not to cry.

"I know," Elizabeth said, reaching out to hug her sister. "Don't worry—we'll get out of here. *Some*how!" She pounded her fists against the door. "Please! Somebody! Let us out!"

A young girl stands behind the closet door, hiding. She watches as a line of bright orange flames crosses the bedroom floor, almost making a circle around the young boy's bed.

Slowly the flames begin to grow higher, inching toward the boy's action-figure comforter.

If they were scared before . . . then this is going to absolutely terrify them, the girl thinks with a wicked smile. Which is exactly the way I want it to be. The more scared they are, the sooner they'll leave my house.

She grins as an orange-blue flame shoots up the edge of the comforter. Amazing, she thinks, that the little boy hasn't woken yet. But some kids will sleep through anything.

Some kids . . . but not me.

Revenge is sweet, Alice, she thinks, staring at the boy's peaceful, unknowing face. Soon his entire bed would be engulfed in flames.

Which was exactly the way she wanted it.

This is going to be so excellent. Steven Wakefield laughed out loud as he revved the motor on the mower he was riding down the sidewalk. Not the huge job of mowing Mrs. Riccoli's lawn—that would probably take him all evening, if he was lucky. But what he was planning to do *before* he mowed the lawn—well, that was another story.

Just a couple of weeks ago he and his best friend, Joe Howell, had come over to "visit" his twin sisters while they baby-sat. He and Joe had been polite about it, Steven thought, chuckling to himself. They'd knocked before entering . . . on the windows, anyway. And they'd worn horrible, scary masks. His sisters had completely freaked. He'd gotten them so good, in fact, they wouldn't even speak to him the whole next day.

Which was a blessing, the way they sometimes talked . . . and talked . . . and talked. About hairstyles. And boys. And anything else that was absurdly silly and juvenile.

Unfortunately his sisters had gone and turned him in to his parents for his last little stunt. His father had wanted Steven to get a part-time job, as his sisters had done, so he would be "responsible," like them. Then his dad had gotten a new riding mower, which had gotten him into even *more* trouble, since he didn't know how to work it.

But that was all over now. He knew how to work the mower, and he planned on making a lot of money over the next month, picking up mowing jobs wherever he could. Mrs. Riccoli was his first client. If he did a good job on her lawn, she'd tell her neighbors, and presto! Steven would be set for life. Or at least until he turned fifteen, when he'd be too old to bother with dumb things like mowing lawns for a living.

Steven gunned the motor, heading for the Riccoli house. Before he started cutting the grass, he had something to take care of. It involved the very scary, gooey, oozing mask he was wearing over his face. With any luck Jessica and Elizabeth would be so busy playing with all those little Riccoli kids that they wouldn't see or hear him drive up. And then he'd show them just how grateful to them he was for ratting on him to their parents.

He'd creep around to the back of the house and look through the window again. The way the twins were acting lately, as if the house were spooked somehow, his gag was guaranteed to turn them into quivering, petrified chickens. He had come at dusk on purpose so they wouldn't be able to see him in the shadows.

But Steven knew he couldn't wait too long— Mrs. Riccoli would probably be getting home soon. And once it got completely dark, he wouldn't be able to see the lawn well enough to mow it.

He pushed the accelerator, cruising toward the house at top speed. The sudden takeoff made his mask slip a little. The gooey strings of fake flesh hung down over the eyeholes.

Steven frantically tried to brush them out of the way, but each time he took a hand off the steering wheel, the mower threatened to lurch out of control. He felt like he'd just grown very long, very irritating hair! *Now I know why girls are always flicking it out of their eyes!* he thought as another giant, thick string of flesh-colored rubber flipped across the right eyehole—and a fake extra eyeball swung down in front, completely covering the left eyehole. Now Steven couldn't see at all!

"Agh!" he cried as the mower crashed through something thick and prickly. The front edge of the mower then hit something rock hard and came abruptly to a stop.

Steven cut the motor and pushed the mask on top of his head. "Phew. OK. So I ran into the house, but nothing really bad happened," he consoled himself, getting off the mower to check the front porch for damage. No broken pieces of wood. No paint scraped off. No giant dents. Nothing.

But there was a strange, acrid smell in the air. Steven wrinkled his nose. A smell like smoke. *Don't tell me I broke the mower!* Steven panicked. He put his nose closer to the mower, sniffing the engine area. But the smoky smell wasn't coming from the mower. Which meant . . . something else must be burning. But what?

Steven turned around and stared up at the house. Why hadn't his sisters come outside when he plowed into it? Wouldn't they have heard the noise?

Suddenly he noticed a thin wisp of dark smoke drifting out of an upstairs window. The house was on fire!

Two

Steven flew into the house, running straight toward the kitchen. "There's always a phone in the kitchen," he muttered to himself, looking around nervously. Where were his sisters? Was everyone outside or something? *Maybe they went to the beach for an evening walk!* he thought, hoping it was true.

Steven flicked on the overhead light in the kitchen. "Aha!" He spotted a cordless phone on the counter, beside a loaf of bread. After quickly dialing 911, he told the dispatcher the Riccolis' address and described the fire. "I don't know how big it is," he said. "I just got here! But hurry!" He slammed down the phone and dashed for the stairs.

Please let everyone be OK! he thought, charging up the stairs two at a time. The upstairs hallway wasn't that smoky. He dashed to the room where the smoke had been coming from. He pressed his hand against the door, and it fell open. Steven gasped. The little boy's bed was surrounded by fire!

"Hey!" Steven yelled, flicking on the light. "Hey, wake up! Are you OK?"

The little boy didn't move. Steven felt his heart pounding. What if the smoke had already gotten into his lungs and . . . *No. I can't let that happen*, Steven told himself, his resolve strengthening.

He quickly slid the scary mask back over his face, hoping it might protect him from the hot flames. Then he jumped toward the bed, yanked off the comforter, and pulled off a wool blanket. He smothered the flames with the blanket, blocking out all the air.

The boy sat up in bed, coughing and rubbing his eyes. "Mommy!" he cried. "Help!"

"It's OK—I've got you," Steven said. "Just hold on a second." He leaped around the bed, putting out all the fire. The floor was slightly scorched, but other than that he seemed to have prevented any serious damage.

"Who—who are you?" the boy asked, peering up at Steven with wide blue eyes. His forehead was creased with worry, and his dark brown hair was sticking out all over the place.

"My name's Steven. It's OK—don't be afraid. I'm Jessica and Elizabeth's big brother," Steven quickly told him, walking around the room to make sure he had gotten all the flames.

The little boy shrank away from Steven, pressing

his back against the headboard of the bed. "But—but—your face . . ."

"Oh, this!" Steven laughed, pulling the mask up off his face. "It's a Halloween mask."

"But it's not Halloween," the boy protested, still looking frightened.

"I know, but I wanted to be ready." Steven grinned at him. "Do you like it?"

"I guess so." Then the boy nodded eagerly. "Yeah! It's cool!"

"Then I'll put it back on," Steven told him with a smile. "OK, now I'm going to pick you up and carry you out of here. There was a fire, and the floor might still be hot," Steven warned. He paused for a moment. "You're not scared of me, are you?"

The boy shook his head. "Not anymore!"

"Good." Steven leaned over the bed and the boy wrapped his arms around his neck. "Now let's get out of this smoky room!" he told the boy. "What's your name?"

"Andrew," the boy said.

"How old are you?" Steven asked.

"I'm eight!" Andrew said proudly.

"Cool," Steven told him, carrying Andrew out into the hallway. "You wait here while I check on your brothers and sisters, OK?" He set Andrew on the top stair. "I'll be right back!"

Steven rushed around the second floor, knocking on doors, making sure everyone was awake. Nobody seemed to be hurt . . . nobody even seemed to have woken up during the fire. Which was fine, except . . . where were his sisters?

"Have any of you guys seen Jessica or Elizabeth lately?" he asked the groggy-looking group of kids assembled by the stairway.

The girl watches, glaring as the boy in the stupid Halloween mask makes sure everyone is all right. How dare he? He doesn't belong there. Now he's ruined everything for her.

She shudders, remembering her utter disgust and disappointment as she watched him put out every last little flame. Not even leaving a chance for the fire to start again. And after all her hard work . . . her planning . . . everyone in the right place at the right time . . . now it's all ruined.

This is something simple for her to fix, however. In fact, there is only one solution to this little problem.

The firefighting boy must die too. It is the only way for her to have what she wants.

And he will die. Soon.

Nobody will get in her way next time. Nobody.

"Did you hear that?" Jessica gasped, her ear pressed tightly against the door.

"Hear what?" Elizabeth asked.

"It sounded like someone yelling," Jessica said. "Maybe somebody came to rescue us!" She wanted more than anything for her guess to be true. But she also knew she was so desperate that the slightest sound might make her think someone had come to save her and Elizabeth. Even the Riccolis' cat meowing might sound like a rescuer at this point.

"I don't hear anything," Elizabeth commented, her ear pressed against the door.

Jessica's heart sank. So she must have been imagining things. "Oh, man," she moaned, burying her face in her hands.

Elizabeth put a firm hand on Jessica's shoulder. "Look, I have an idea."

Jessica glanced at Elizabeth through her fingers. "You do?"

Elizabeth nodded. "We're going to back up and run straight at the door. On the count of three we *both* kick down the door."

Jessica wrinkled her nose. "That door is pretty heavy—"

"Jess, it's our only chance," Elizabeth insisted.

Jessica took a deep breath, trying to pull herself together. "OK. I'm ready."

"Good," Elizabeth said, and led Jessica a few steps back, toward the window. "Here we go. One . . . two . . . three!" she yelled.

Jessica charged straight at the door. She and Elizabeth kicked at the same instant—and to Jessica's amazement, the door burst open!

"We did it!" Elizabeth shrieked as they crashed into the hallway, knocking the door back against the wall.

"Yes!" Jessica cried, giving Elizabeth a quick high five before they both turned and made a bee-line for the stairs.

The only problem was the circular, winding stairs

were wide enough for one person at a time—and Elizabeth was trying to run down right beside her. "Elizabeth, get out of the—"

Before Jessica could finish her sentence, she had tripped over Elizabeth, and they both went tumbling down the stairs. They landed in a heap at the bottom.

"Elizabeth," Jessica said, moaning in pain as she got to her feet, rubbing her bruised shins. "We can't both run down . . . down . . ." she sputtered, staring at the figure in front of her.

A gruesome face with strings of dripping flesh hanging over its eyes was looking right at her!

Three

That looks just like the monster from Jessica's nightmare! Elizabeth thought, panicking. "Jessica—is that—"

"I don't know what it is, but we're going to get it!" Jessica hissed.

Elizabeth looked from the monster to the five kids assembled in the hallway, hardly knowing what to do first. "You guys are all right?" she asked uncertainly. "Nobody's hurt from the fire?"

"Or from . . . that thing?" Jessica asked, pointing to the monster.

It took a step toward them, and Elizabeth lunged at the figure, tackling it to the ground. "Don't even think about it!" she yelled.

Jessica landed squarely on top of Elizabeth, pressing down with her weight. "OK, we've got you!" she yelled. "So don't do anything stupid!"

Underneath her Elizabeth heard a muffled cry for help. "Mmmph," the monster groaned. Something about its voice seemed very familiar.

Elizabeth pressed down even harder, flattening the figure to the floor, pressing its gory face into the hallway carpet. "Mmmph-thpt!" it mumbled.

"Fight, fight!" Andrew cheered, jumping up and down.

"Go, Elizabeth!" Juliana, who was five, added in a boisterous shriek. "Get him!"

"Him?" Elizabeth mumbled. *But wait a second. Wasn't the monster in everyone's dreams a girl?* She craned her neck to look over her shoulder at Jessica. "Shouldn't we be getting *her*?"

The body trapped beneath them suddenly let out a groan. "It's me, you idiots!"

"You?" Elizabeth glanced at her sister. Both girls released their hold on the monster, who stood up and pulled off a gory, gooey mask to reveal . . .

Elizabeth glared at her brother. Her heart was beating double time from the shock of fighting what she *thought* was a monster. And now it was Steven instead?

Jessica stood up, brushing carpet lint off her shirt. "What in the world are you doing here, and *why* were you wearing that horrendous mask?"

"Wait a second," Elizabeth said, getting to her feet. "Don't tell me you came by to scare us again!" She pressed her index finger into Steven's chest.

Jessica stared at the mask in Steven's hand. "If

you did, I will personally tear that dumb mask into a million pieces. And you're next!"

"I mean, what were you thinking?" Elizabeth asked. "Scaring us, scaring the kids—"

Andrew grinned happily. "With that mask on, he was so cool. He looked just like—like—"

Great. Now Andrew thinks Steven's cool! Elizabeth thought. Never mind that the phony monster had practically given her a heart attack.

"He looked like that Frankenstein monster!" cried Gretchen, the seven-year-old. "Only you forgot to put the bolts in your neck," she told Steven, giggling.

"Actually I kind of forgot about this silly thing," Steven admitted, sheepishly glancing at the mask in his hand.

"Yeah, I'm *sure* you did," Jessica said, her arms folded squarely across her chest.

"Right after you scared us half to death!" Elizabeth added, glaring at Steven. She grabbed the mask out of his hand and held it up in front of his face. "And I know Mom and Dad are going to love hearing about this!"

"Good move, Elizabeth. Now we have *evidence*." Jessica raised her eyebrows. "Not to mention several witnesses, who will swear they saw you try to ambush us wearing that."

"You can pretty much count on being grounded for the next six months," Elizabeth said, still clutching the mask as she folded her arms.

"Uh-oh," Olivia said, bouncing Nate, who was

two, on her knee. "Steven's in trouble!"

"Twouble!" Nate exclaimed, pointing at Steven.

"Who knows . . . maybe this time Dad will make you clean out the garage, or Mom will have you mop the kitchen floor . . . and the basement. . . ." Jessica tapped her chin with her fingers. "The possibilities are endless, really."

Steven nervously cleared his throat. "Well, me trying to scare you guys isn't really the point now, is it? I mean, the point is, I got here in time to put out the fire and save everyone. Speaking of which . . . where *were* you guys when I got here, anyway?"

"Long story," Jessica whispered under her breath. "We'll tell you later."

Elizabeth looked at all the kids, sitting safely in the hall, and smiled. She didn't smell smoke anymore, and it was obvious that they were all out of danger. She felt the tension slowly drain out of her. Everything was going to be OK. "Did you really put out the fire?" she asked Steven.

"Of course! Ask Andrew," Steven told her.

Elizabeth turned to the little boy, who was crouched beside Steven. "Is it true? Did Steven help you?"

Andrew nodded. "He came running into my room and put out the fire, then he grabbed me and carried me out! Just like Superman would!"

Elizabeth looked at her brother. She couldn't help feeling at least a little bit proud of him. Steven could be a jerk sometimes, but he was basically an OK person.

"Just like Superman . . . what can I say?" Steven flexed his biceps.

"Actually I think Gretchen was right—you're more like Frankenstein's monster!" Jessica teased.

"Uh-uh," Andrew argued. "That monster's afraid of fire. But not Steven. He rescued me!"

"Please," Elizabeth said, resting her hand on Andrew's shoulder. "Don't encourage him *too* much."

"So the fire was in your room?" Jessica asked Andrew, pulling him to his feet. "How did that happen?"

Jessica had a feeling she already knew the answer to that question, but she wanted to hear Andrew admit it. Just a few days ago there had been another small fire, and Mrs. Riccoli had told her and Elizabeth that Andrew had a history of playing with matches.

"I don't know how it happened," Andrew said with an innocent shrug. "I was asleep."

"Oh, really?" Jessica asked, putting her hands on her hips.

"Really!" Andrew insisted. "I'm telling the truth!"

"Well . . ." Jessica studied the little boy's face. He did seem pretty sincere. "How about if we go check it out anyway?"

"Yeah, I want to make sure the fire's completely gone," Elizabeth added, following them down the hall toward the front of the house.

"It's gone," Steven assured them. "But I guess a second look wouldn't hurt."

Olivia, still carrying Nate, and Juliana and Gretchen all came along too.

"Now, everyone be careful," Jessica instructed the group, pausing in the doorway. "Don't touch anything—"

She broke off as she heard the squeal of a siren— then another siren, and a loud honk, and the roar of an engine barreling up the driveway.

Steven dashed into Andrew's room and peered out the window. "The fire trucks are here!"

"Well, duh," Jessica said, rolling her eyes. "Who did you think it was? A pizza delivery?"

"Did you call them?" Elizabeth asked, standing beside her brother at the window.

"As soon as I got here and saw the smoke," Steven said. "I figured we might need help."

"Whoo-hoo! Fire trucks!" Andrew screamed excitedly. He sprinted down the stairs to meet them, along with the other kids.

Jessica hurried to follow them—she wanted to tell the firefighters they had nothing to worry about.

She was halfway down the stairs when the front door burst open and six yellow-coated figures sprinted up toward her. "It's OK! The fire's out—" she tried to say, but they barreled right past her, almost knocking her down.

Jessica took a second to collect herself. Wanting to rescue her was one thing, but being completely rude about it was another! Did they teach manners at firefighting school or what?

She went downstairs to wait with the kids. "Could you believe the nerve of those guys?" she commented to Elizabeth, who was holding Andrew's hand to keep him from running upstairs.

"Well, it is their job," Elizabeth pointed out.

"Did you expect them to chat with you first?" Steven laughed.

"If they had, I could have told them there was nothing to worry about," Jessica declared.

"We don't think so, anyway," Elizabeth said. "But it's their job to make sure."

"Whatever." Jessica shook her head. If they wanted to waste time looking around, she wouldn't stop them. Then a thought occurred to her. If they checked the entire house . . .

Jessica took a step closer to her sister. "Elizabeth? Should we tell them about . . . you know. The bedroom, on the third floor."

"I guess they'll find it on their own," Elizabeth said. "I don't know. We left the door open."

"We left the door off its hinges," Jessica amended. "Do you think Mrs. Riccoli will notice? Or should we tell her we did it?"

"She has enough on her mind—especially now that Andrew seems to be playing with matches again," Elizabeth commented with a concerned glance at Andrew.

A few minutes later the firefighters strolled back downstairs. "Looks like you kids took care of everything," the tallest one said, taking off his helmet. He had sandy blond hair, and he looked to Jessica like he was about twenty years old. "But we did a thorough safety check anyway. Seems to have been a very localized fire."

"Can we ride on your truck?" Andrew asked, peering up at him.

Funny, Jessica thought, gazing at the firefighter's gorgeous face. *I was just about to ask the same thing!*

"Not today, son." The firefighter slipped his helmet over Andrew's head. "We can't stick around long." He looked at Jessica. "Are your parents anywhere close by?"

Jessica felt like she was going to faint. He had the brightest blue eyes she had ever seen. "Parents?" she repeated, staring at him. *Do I even have parents? I can't remember.*

"Actually we're the baby-sitters," Elizabeth explained. "My name's Elizabeth, and this is Jessica. And this is our brother, Steven—he's the one who called."

The firefighter nodded. "I'm Ryan Locke, the captain. And we're very glad you're all right. Mind if we go outside and talk?"

"Mind?" Jessica asked. *Is he kidding?* "Of course not." She followed Ryan out onto the front porch. *Ryan Locke. He even has a perfect name to go with his perfect face.*

Jessica walked outside. She glanced over at the driveway, where a few firefighters were giving the kids a tour of the fire truck. *Now, if I could just send*

Elizabeth and Steven over there too, Ryan and I would be all alone. . . .

Ryan leaned against the porch railing. "Any idea how this started?"

Jessica flicked her blond hair over her shoulder. "Actually *I* have an idea."

"You do?" Ryan looked at her attentively. "Tell me."

"Well, I—I . . ." Jessica faltered. Having Ryan look at her like that had made her forget her idea!

"Yes?" Ryan prompted.

Look away, Jessica told herself, *or you'll end up sounding like a complete fool!* She turned her head slightly, gazing behind Ryan at the driveway.

That was when she saw it. Mrs. Riccoli's blue minivan—heading up the driveway at top speed!

Uh-oh, she thought, smiling nervously at Ryan.

Elizabeth hurried over to assure Mrs. Riccoli that everything was all right.

Mrs. Riccoli threw open the minivan's door and leaped out of the car. She rushed right past Elizabeth as if she didn't even see her. She ran to the fire truck, where her kids were gathered in a semicircle, listening to a female firefighter.

"Now, if you ever smell smoke again," the firefighter was telling the group, "you kids know what to do, right?"

Without saying a word to anyone, Mrs. Riccoli ran around the circle, breathlessly tapping each of her children on the head. "Nate, Juliana, Gretchen, Andrew, Olivia," she chanted.

"Duck, duck, goose!" Nate cried. He took off and started running around the circle, trying to tap everyone on the back of the knee.

Mrs. Riccoli laughed nervously, bending down to scoop Nate into her arms. "You're all OK?" she asked. "What *happened*?" Her forehead was creased with worry.

"Everyone's fine," Elizabeth assured her. "Nobody was hurt. And the fire was small."

"But . . . how?" Mrs. Riccoli stared at Elizabeth, confused. "Did something happen in the kitchen?"

"It wasn't a kitchen fire," Ryan, the fire captain, told her. "The fire occurred upstairs in one of the bedrooms."

"Andrew's bedroom, to be exact," Elizabeth filled in. "But—we saved him just in time." She glanced at Steven, hoping he wouldn't let on that he'd been the one who came to Andrew's rescue. She didn't want to explain that she and Jessica were locked in a secret bedroom—not with so many people around. Besides, all Mrs. Riccoli needed to know right now was that her kids were fine.

"In Andrew's bedroom?" Mrs. Riccoli gasped.

"Everything's all right. Let's go upstairs and have a little talk," Ryan suggested, taking Mrs. Riccoli's arm and gently guiding her into the house. "Come on, everyone."

Jessica hurried to follow him. Elizabeth took Juliana's hand and they all trooped back up to Andrew's room. Some slightly browned wood on the bedroom floor was almost the only evidence that anything had happened.

"The fire started on the floor, beside his bed," Ryan explained. "And it had just caught onto his comforter when your baby-sitters came in and put it out with this blanket here." He held up the blue blanket and nodded at Elizabeth and Jessica. "Good thinking."

Andrew's eyes widened as he pointed at Steven. "It was—"

Jessica grabbed his arm and beamed at Ryan Locke. "Well, I knew that was the right thing to do. Call it good instincts, I guess."

Steven rolled his eyes. "Don't push your luck," he muttered under his breath.

"Andrew . . . he was so close . . ." Mrs. Riccoli's face turned ashen. She stared at the burned corner of the comforter, which was crumpled on the ground. Then she crouched down, looking Andrew right in the face. "Honey, how many times do I have to tell you? Matches are nothing to play with. Do you understand what could have happened to you today? To everybody?"

"But I didn't do anything," Andrew protested, his mouth turned down in a pout. "I didn't!"

"It doesn't do any good to lie about it either," Mrs. Riccoli said sternly. "Now, this is the absolute last time you are ever going to touch a match—do you hear me?"

"But Mom," Andrew began, stomping his foot on the floor.

"But nothing." Mrs. Riccoli gathered him in her

arms. "I can't let anything happen to you, sweetie. Ever. Don't you know that?"

"Something doesn't add up here," Steven whispered. "Come on." He beckoned Elizabeth out of the bedroom into the hallway while the others examined the fire damage.

Elizabeth gave her brother a questioning look. "What do you mean?" she asked in a soft voice. "What doesn't add up?"

"Well, Andrew *couldn't* have started the fire." Steven shook his head.

"He couldn't have? Why not?" Elizabeth asked.

"Because. When I got to his room, he was still asleep," Steven told her. "He didn't wake up until I yelled at him."

Elizabeth tried to picture the scene. "Well, he could have left a lit match on the floor before he went to sleep . . . or maybe he thought it was out, only it wasn't."

Steven looked skeptical. "Maybe. But he sounds pretty sure about not playing with matches in the first place."

Elizabeth glanced back through the doorway at Andrew, who was still protesting. He didn't seem like the kind of kid who would lie to his mother about something that important.

But if he hadn't started the fire, then who—or what—had?

Elizabeth had no idea. But she couldn't help thinking it had something to do with those horrible dreams everyone kept having. *This house* is *haunted,* she thought, glancing at the stairs to the third floor. *Definitely haunted.*

"So where were you guys, anyway?" Steven asked. "You never told me."

Elizabeth bit her lip. Her legs were shaking. "We were upstairs," she told Steven. "We went into this secret bedroom up there and the door closed. We couldn't get out."

"Serves you right for snooping around, I guess," Steven said with a shrug.

Normally Elizabeth would have argued with him. But she had a sudden feeling that what had happened that night wasn't just a coincidence. She and Jessica were trapped while someone set a fire downstairs . . . someone who wasn't Andrew.

So who was it? And why did he or she want to hurt all of them?

Steven leaned against the porch railing, watching the fire truck's lights disappear down the driveway. It was almost completely dark now. "Well, I'd better take off. I'll come back tomorrow to work on your lawn."

"We'll go with you," Jessica said. "I mean, if that's OK with you." She looked at Mrs. Riccoli.

"Sure. It's fine," Mrs. Riccoli said, peering out at the lawn.

"Are you OK?" Elizabeth asked. "You seem kind of distracted. Do you want us to stick around and help watch the kids for a while?"

Mrs. Riccoli shook her head. "No, I'm not worried about that. The fire's out and Captain Locke told me the house is safe. But I am wondering about one thing. . . ." She walked to the edge of the porch, staring out at the yard. "What in the world happened to my *hedge*?"

Steven followed Mrs. Riccoli's gaze. He could just barely make out a hedge—with a giant, person-size hole right in the middle of it! Steven felt his stomach knot. Somehow he'd managed to forget crashing into something like a prickly wall right before he hit the house. *Oops.*

"Oh . . . that?" he asked. "Gee, how did that happen?" He flashed Mrs. Riccoli a nervous, innocent smile.

"I wonder," Elizabeth said. "I'm sure you didn't have anything to do with it."

"Hey, I was too busy rushing to the house to help *you* guys to do any yard work," Steven said in self-defense. "I mean, all I did was park, and then I saw the smoke, and—well, you know the rest." He cleared his throat.

"Uh-huh." Jessica nodded. "So you didn't have anything to do with it."

"No, of course not." Steven shook his head. Then he got an idea. He wasn't the only person who'd come rushing up to the house that night. He snapped his fingers. "I know! I bet the *fire* truck did it. They were in a big hurry and—"

Mrs. Riccoli laughed, interrupting him. "Steven, even in the *dark* I can see that hole over there wasn't made by a truck. In fact, it's precisely the size and shape of you sitting on that mower."

"Is it really?" Steven smiled. "Well . . . uh . . . did I mention that Howell and Wakefield Landscaping specializes in hedge replacement?"

At least . . . we do now.

Four

"Elizabeth, I've decided something, and you can't talk me out of it." Jessica marched up to the kitchen counter and poured herself a glass of orange juice.

"What is it?" Elizabeth asked, looking up at her sister and sleepily rubbing her eyes. She couldn't believe Jessica had so much energy. Baby-sitting the night before had wiped Elizabeth out. She felt like she was going to sleep through every single one of her Friday morning classes.

"I'll sum it up in three words." Jessica pulled back a chair and sat down at the table. "Read my lips, Elizabeth. *No more baby-sitting!*"

Elizabeth stared at her twin, shocked. "No more baby-sitting? As in, ever?"

"As in, I am not going back to Mrs. Riccoli's house," Jessica declared. "I can't take it! The fire thing, that weird secret bedroom, having that awful nightmare—it's like being in the middle of a long, horrible scary movie whenever we're there. I'm calling her today to tell her I'm quitting."

"Qu-Quitting?" Elizabeth stuttered. "But—what about the kids? They really love you—they're attached to you. You can't just leave them like that." She imagined the look on little Nate's face if she had to tell him Jessica wasn't coming back to see him. He'd be heartbroken.

"Why not?" Jessica shrugged. "There are plenty of other baby-sitters in town, including half our friends. Anyway, I want to have a social life. You remember what that is, don't you?"

"Well, sure. Actually . . ." Elizabeth bit her lip. Maria Slater, one of her best friends, had invited her to a big sleepover party for that very night. But Elizabeth had promised to baby-sit, so she'd had to tell Maria no. Maria had teased Elizabeth about being so busy working that she never had time for anything fun anymore. "But baby-sitting's fun," she'd argued to Maria. At least it had been fun, at the very beginning. Now? Elizabeth had spent the whole night before being scared out of her wits. "Of course I want to have a social life too," she told her sister. "And I want to leave that . . . house too. But Jessica, we can't just abandon those kids." Elizabeth had never walked away in the middle of a job before, for any reason.

"We're not *abandoning* them," Jessica protested.

"We're just . . . turning them over to other people who are just as great at baby-sitting as we are." She calmly dropped a slice of bread into the toaster. "It's not like we can't *visit* them. We're just not going to baby-sit them all the time. . . . I mean, Elizabeth, it's not like we're making *that* much money."

"We're not?" Elizabeth asked. The fact was, she'd never made so much money before in her life. She'd even treated her entire group of friends to ice cream a couple of days ago, she was feeling so rich.

Jessica considered it for a minute. "OK. Maybe we are making a lot of money. But that's why we can afford to take some time off!" Her toast popped up, and she started buttering it. "Listen, if we quit now—and don't try to talk me out of it anymore, because *my* mind's made up—just think about it. No more freaky stuff happening, no more fires, no more nightmares . . . I mean, for all we know, *we're* the ones jinxing the place and making all that strange stuff happen."

"Well . . . it's true that Mrs. Riccoli seems perfectly fine. And nothing's happened to any of our friends who are baby-sitting for her," Elizabeth said, thinking it over. Amy Sutton, Todd Wilkins, and Winston Egbert all baby-sat for the Riccolis, and none of them had reported anything really freaky happening yet.

Elizabeth had to admit, her sister had a point. Jessica had the horrible nightmare. And they'd both been stuck in that secret bedroom . . . and then there was the fire. Elizabeth *was* a little uncomfortable about the idea of going back to the Riccolis'. Still, she didn't want to leave Mrs. Riccoli in the lurch, without enough baby-sitters. "Do you think maybe we could take a few days off or something instead?" she suggested to Jessica.

"A few days off? Try a month," Jessica declared. "You can go back if you want, but I've had enough of that house. It gives me the creeps." She shuddered, taking a bite of toast.

"What gives you the creeps?"

Elizabeth looked up to see her mother standing in the kitchen doorway. "Oh, hi, Mom," she said, smiling. She'd been so caught up in her thoughts that she hadn't even heard her mother's footsteps.

"Good morning." Mrs. Wakefield picked up a mug from the counter and took a sip. "Mmm. Nothing like a little cold coffee to get you going in the morning." She made a face. "Now, what were you saying about having the creeps?"

"Oh, uh—nothing, really," Jessica said quickly, shooting Elizabeth a look.

Elizabeth knew what Jessica meant. They didn't want to worry their mother. Especially if they weren't even going back to the Riccolis'. *Why does that idea make me so happy?* Elizabeth wondered. *And how can I even think about quitting? I guess because deep down, I really want to—just like Jessica does.*

"What's so creepy is the scary thought that if I keep baby-sitting so much, everyone at school's going to think I fell off the planet or something," Jessica explained to their mother. "I mean, I haven't been to a party in, like, a year."

"A few weeks, I think," Mrs. Wakefield corrected her, smiling.

"Whatever," Jessica said with a wave of her hand. "But here's my plan, Mom. Good-bye, baby-sitting, hello, social life!" She grinned.

"Sounds good to me," Mrs. Wakefield agreed, nodding. "I think you two have both earned some time off. Don't you, Elizabeth?"

Elizabeth sighed. "Well, I guess so. I mean, there's this sleepover party tonight that I really wanted to go to," she said slowly, already feeling excited about spending time with her friends. A sleepover sounded a lot more fun right now than going back to the Riccolis'. "Maybe we should tell Mrs. Riccoli we need some time for ourselves—"

"Maybe nothing!" Jessica practically leaped out of her chair. "And right after I call her, I've got to call Lila and see what I've missed! Which is only about half of the entire *year*."

Elizabeth laughed. "You're going to see Lila at school this morning, remember? Why do you have to call her?"

Jessica shot her an incredulous look. "Elizabeth, you just don't know what it's like to have an incredibly busy social life."

*   *   *

Alice Wakefield sat at the breakfast table, watching Jessica and Elizabeth walk down the sidewalk on their way to school. She'd tried to hide her relief at the news that they wouldn't be going back to the Riccoli house. Her daughters didn't need to know that she too had been a baby-sitter at that house. A long time ago . . .

Alice was sitting downstairs in the Sullivans' house, reading a novel for her sophomore English class, when she heard a shriek upstairs. Oh, no, *she thought.* Not another one of Eva's nightmares!

Alice closed her book and hurried for the stairs, dashing up to Eva's bedroom. Eva had nightmares frequently, and she was also prone to walking in her sleep. But if Eva was the most difficult child Alice baby-sat for, she could also be one of the sweetest.

Alice ran into Eva's bedroom on the third floor and shook the little girl awake. "It's OK, it's OK," she told Eva gently, putting her hand on the little girl's arm.

"But—it was terrible," Eva said, shivering. "I dreamed that it was Halloween!"

Alice smiled, brushing a few tendrils of Eva's long red hair off her cheek. "Well, what's so terrible about Halloween? Didn't you have fun last year?"

Eva shook her head. "No. I was sick and my mom wouldn't let me trick or treat."

"You're not sick this year," Alice pointed out. "And you're going to have a great time, I promise. Halloween's one of the greatest holidays of the entire year. And it's

not really scary—except in a fun kind of way. Because
all your friends have creepy costumes, but you know
that underneath, it's only your friends."

"But—in my dream I was running and running
from the creepy, scary monster. It wasn't a costume, it
was real! And she grabbed my ankle and—"

"Don't think about it!" Alice said. "Just forget you
even dreamed that." She knew she was repeating herself—she told Eva the same thing practically every
night. But it usually helped calm her down. Alice
figured that Eva would eventually outgrow the
nightmares. Until then it was her job to apply damage
control. "Remember what I told you, Eva? Nightmares
are just . . . silly things that happen when we're
asleep. They have nothing to do with what's really
going to happen. Your dreams can't hurt you—no
matter how real they seem. No matter how scared you
are, you'll always wake up."

Eva looked up, her eyes full of doubt.

"Really," Alice said. "You can trust me." She reached
out to hug Eva, but the little girl's hug was hesitant, as
though she wasn't convinced.

"So, how many hours did it take to you to fix the
Riccolis' hedge?" Joe asked with a smirk, flopping
onto Steven's bed late Friday afternoon.

Steven frowned at him. He didn't see what
was so funny about him running into that dumb
hedge the night before. If the fire engine had run
it over, nobody would have cared. And wasn't
that what he'd been—a firefighter? The one who

rescued everybody, by putting out the flames? But no. Instead of getting a medal, he'd had to spend thirty dollars of his hard-earned cash buying a new hedge.

"Forget about the hedge," Steven said. "What we need now are some new clients. I'm completely broke."

"But didn't Mrs. Riccoli pay you for mowing—"

Steven glared at him, one eyebrow raised. "Yeah. And it almost covered the cost of the new hedge. OK? Are you through?"

"Jeez. Touchy." Joe smiled and punched the pillow on the bed. "Well, we put up all those signs at the grocery store. Someone has to read one eventually."

"Eventually?" Steven scoffed. "What am I supposed to do until—"

Just then the telephone in the hallway rang. Steven practically leaped across his bedroom in one step to answer it. If his sisters picked it up first, he might as well kiss his business good-bye!

"Howell and Wakefield Landscaping," he said in a deep voice.

"Yes," a man's voice replied. "I'm calling about your ad."

"Our ad?" Steven turned to Joe, giving him a thumbs-up. "Yes, of course. Well, how can we help you today?"

"I've just moved into a new house, and I'm afraid the grounds have been horribly neglected," the man said. "My name's Taylor Morgan, by the way."

Taylor Morgan—that's a rich person's name, Steven thought, dollar signs dancing in front of his eyes. *Grounds? Did he say grounds?* As far as he knew, only rich people called their lawn "grounds"—it meant they had more than one lawn. "So you need some general cleanup, mowing, weeding, et cetera?" Steven asked. "Of your *grounds*?" *To the tune of, say, a hundred dollars an hour?*

"Exactly," Mr. Morgan replied. "But I'm afraid . . . well, we're having a last-minute housewarming party on Sunday, and I'd need everything done by then. Is there any way you could come over this afternoon and take a look? Of course, I'm still at work—I won't be there. But my daughter can show you around."

"Well, let me check my schedule. . . ." Steven grabbed a few pieces of paper off the notepad by the phone and rustled them around loudly in front of the mouthpiece. Really important, busy people made a lot of rustling noises when they sorted through all the papers on their desks. He'd seen his dad do it at his law office. "Yes, I think that would be possible. We could be over in, oh . . . fifteen minutes, actually."

"Terrific! It's 207 Larkspur Way—you know, the attractive little cul-de-sac over by the beach?" Mr. Morgan asked.

Steven jotted down the address. Not that he even knew what a cul-de-whatever was, but he was sure he could find it. "Yes, sir. We'll check it out and get started right away." Steven hung up the phone.

"Yes! We're employed!" he shouted triumphantly, giving Joe a high five. "Let's go!"

They took the stairs down three at a time and burst out the front door.

"So this guy has a lot of money to spend?" Joe asked as they headed down the sidewalk in the general direction of the beach.

Steven nodded. "From the sound of things, he's loaded."

"Cool," Joe said, starting to jog. "Just *don't* mess it up this time."

"Me mess it up?" Steven replied. "What about you? What about the time you ran out of gas in the middle of—"

"Excuse me, but at least *I* never ran down a hedge," Joe retorted, giving Steven a gentle shove off the curb.

"I told you, it was an emergency!" Steven said.

"Yeah. The hedge almost died!" Joe replied, laughing.

"Ha ha, very funny," Steven muttered. Of course, he couldn't expect Joe to understand how hard he'd worked just to get them this job. That Mr. Morgan could have easily chosen someone else to handle his *grounds* if Steven hadn't sounded so professional on the telephone. Joe wasn't half as grateful as he ought to be. Without Steven around to help, Joe would be bagging groceries for the rest of his life!

Well, we can't all be business geniuses. I guess it's a burden I'll have to live with! Steven chuckled to himself.

*   *   *

Jessica stretched her arms over her head, shifting slightly on the couch in the living room. She was vaguely aware that her brother and his friend Joe had just run out of the house. But whatever Steven was up to, it couldn't be even half as interesting as what was going on in Granville, the setting for *The Guilty and the Glamorous.* Jessica had been so busy baby-sitting, she'd missed an entire two weeks of her new favorite TV soap opera, which came on right after her *old* favorite, *Days of Turmoil*, which was extremely convenient.

Fortunately the plot hadn't changed much in the two weeks since she'd last seen it. Everyone was still at the same fancy ball they'd been at the last time she watched. Only they seemed to be leaving the giant, fancy party, or at least starting to *think* about leaving. Coats were being discussed, anyway.

Jessica smiled as the most handsome man on the show, Briggs, held out a coat for Geneva, the character she liked best of all. Geneva had long blond hair, like Jessica, and she was always getting the best boyfriends.

"May I offer you a ride home?" Briggs asked Geneva politely.

"How about if we go to the Downtown Café for a cappuccino first?" Geneva replied. "A little coffee would hit the spot. I'm exhausted, but I would love to hear more about your new cosmetics firm. After all, if I'm going to be the spokesmodel for it—"

"Which you most certainly are," Briggs said, carefully taking Geneva's hand.

Brrrinnngg! The telephone beside the couch jolted Jessica back to reality. She wasn't in Granville . . . she wasn't at the fancy party or going out for a cappuccino with Briggs. . . .

Well, maybe it's Lila with some kind of plan, anyway, she thought, lifting the receiver to her ear. "Hello?"

"Oh, Elizabeth! Or is that Jessica?" a very flustered-sounding Mrs. Riccoli asked.

"It's Jessica. What's wrong?" She'd never heard Mrs. Riccoli sound so upset.

Mrs. Riccoli sniffled a few times, then burst into tears.

"Oh, no!" Jessica cried, panic rising in her chest. "Mrs. Riccoli, what is it? What's happened? It's not—it's not Nate, is it? Or Andrew? Was there another fire or—"

"I'm sorry, Jessica," Mrs. Riccoli broke in. "I didn't mean to fall apart on you like that, but I've just been trying to keep it all inside and—well, you see, something very unfortunate has happened. My mother has had a heart attack, and I've simply got to visit her in the hospital. Right away."

"That's terrible! I'm so sorry," Jessica said quickly. "She's . . . doing OK now, though?"

"She's resting, but she wants to see me. Which means I need to get out of here as soon as I can," Mrs. Riccoli explained. "Do you think there's any way you and Elizabeth could come watch the kids while I visit her?"

Jessica drummed her fingernails against the arm of the couch. She didn't want to go back to that creepy house, not for anything. But this was an emergency. Mrs. Riccoli needed her. "Well, OK, sure," Jessica told her. "We could come over for a couple of hours this afternoon." *But not any longer than that!*

"Oh, no. I'm afraid you've misunderstood, or else I forgot to mention this," Mrs. Riccoli said, "but my mother lives in *Florida*."

"F-Florida?" Jessica sputtered.

"Yes, Florida," Mrs. Riccoli continued, sounding breathless. "So you see, I'll need to be gone for the whole weekend at least. My husband is going to fly from Sacramento and meet me down in Florida. And I know it's short notice, and I know you wanted to give up baby-sitting, but I was thinking, between you and Elizabeth and the rest of the gang—maybe you could stay here? I'd pay you double, triple, whatever you think is fair, but the thing is, I've got to go now, this afternoon, because if I don't, well, who knows what might—"

"Mrs. Riccoli, it's all right!" Jessica cut in. No matter how she felt about baby-sitting at that house, somebody had to help Mrs. Riccoli. Jessica didn't mind coming to the rescue. Actually she kind of liked the image of herself as the type of person who would save the day. A real heroine type.

"Of course you need us. And you don't have to worry about a thing! We'll do it. We'll be over there in . . . half an hour."

"Oh, Jessica—you're an angel!" Mrs. Riccoli exclaimed, starting to cry all over again.

A few minutes later Jessica hung up the phone. *Mrs. Riccoli actually called me an angel. No one's ever called me that before.*

Of course, she had a feeling Elizabeth was going to call her something else entirely when she broke the news about their staying at the Riccolis' house that night. But she also knew that if Elizabeth had been the one who answered the phone, she would have promised Mrs. Riccoli the very same thing. How could they say no? Poor Mrs. Riccoli—her mother was so sick!

Jessica got off the couch and walked upstairs. She paused in the doorway to her sister's room.

Elizabeth was neatly folding her favorite pair of pajamas. She placed them in her small blue duffel bag, then zipped the bag closed. "Well, all I need is my toothbrush and I'll be set," she said cheerfully, heading for the bathroom. "What are you doing tonight?"

Jessica followed her, trying to figure out the best way to break the news. "Well, I thought I was going to a movie with the Unicorns," she began. "But something else just came up."

"Really? What?" Elizabeth asked, sliding her toothbrush into a pink plastic case. "A party?"

"No, not exactly," Jessica stalled. "Uh . . . remember what I said this morning, about how I wanted to quit baby-sitting and how we were never going back to the Riccolis'?" Jessica asked. "Could you, like, *forget* that I ever said that?" She flashed Elizabeth her sweetest smile.

Five

Elizabeth crouched over the handlebars of her bike, pumping her legs up and down, riding as fast as she could. Of course, it wasn't easy, with a large duffel bag on her back. The bag she was *supposed* to be taking to Maria's house. Only she was going to the Riccolis' house instead.

Not that she was mad at Mrs. Riccoli. How could she be, after Jessica explained the reason they had to fill in as emergency baby-sitters for the weekend? It wasn't Mrs. Riccoli's fault that Elizabeth had gotten so excited about hanging out with her friends and staying up all night at Maria's sleepover. It was Jessica's.

"Looks like it's going to rain tonight," Jessica commented, riding beside her. "What do you think?"

Elizabeth glanced at her briefly, then focused on

the street again. She knew it was kind of childish, but she didn't plan on speaking to Jessica until she absolutely had to.

"I hope it doesn't," Jessica went on. "Because it's totally going to ruin my plans for giving the kids a picnic dinner on the lawn. That is, if Steven left any grass for us to play on." She giggled and looked at Elizabeth, as if waiting for her to join in the fun. Elizabeth normally enjoyed jokes about Steven, but right now she didn't feel like laughing. That morning, after Jessica had convinced her not to go back to the Riccolis', Elizabeth had finally felt safe and free. And now here she was, heading back to the Riccoli house!

"Come on, Elizabeth—you can't ignore everything I say for the entire night!" Jessica argued.

Elizabeth only pedaled faster. *Just watch me!* she thought.

All of a sudden Jessica burst out laughing.

Elizabeth glared at her. "What's so funny?"

"*You* are," Jessica managed to get out in between giggles. "You're all hunched over and riding so fast . . . you know who you look like? The Wicked Witch in *The Wizard of Oz*—only you forgot Toto!" Laughing, Jessica crouched over her handlebars and pedaled ahead, singing the soundtrack to the movie.

Watching her from behind, Elizabeth felt a small smile creeping up at the corners of her mouth. *OK. Maybe I can't give Jessica the silent treatment forever.* After all, Elizabeth knew that she and Jessica would have to stick together in order to make it through the night.

Elizabeth switched gears and worked extra hard to catch up to Jessica. "You're not even doing it right," she said, coasting beside her. "Her back is more hunched over—like this!" She bent over in her best imitation of the Wicked Witch.

"Hello, we're—" Steven's words caught in his throat as the front door to the Morgans' house swung open.

Standing there, wearing cutoff blue jean shorts and a neon green bikini top, was the most beautiful girl he had ever seen. She had long blond hair, golden brown skin . . . not to mention the most attractive feet Steven had ever seen. He stared at her sandals. He'd never even thought of feet as having looks before—but hers were amazing.

"Yes?" she asked. "You're *who*?"

Steven looked up at her face and smiled nervously. "We're from—" He paused, lowering his voice an octave or two. How was he supposed to talk to the girl of his dreams? What words were there? "We're from Howell and Wakefield Landscaping. I'm Howell—" *Agh. Say anything but that, you idiot!*

"He's Wakefield," Joe corrected him, patting Steven on the back. "He's been out in the sun a little too long—gets confused, you know."

Steven glared at him, shrugging Joe's hand off his shoulder. "I'm totally fine, actually."

"*I'm* Howell. Joe, that is." Joe held out his hand. "Nice to meet you . . . ?"

"Karen Morgan," the girl said, briefly shaking Joe's hand. She flicked her hair over her shoulder, and Steven saw an expensive-looking watch on her wrist—the kind professional scuba divers wore.

Steven tried to forget about the fact that he had run out the door wearing last year's cool T-shirt and a nondescript pair of baggy jeans. Or that his plastic watch came from a box of Sugar Shocker cereal. "I'm Steven," he said, putting on what he hoped was a cool, studly grin. "Wakefield."

"OK, well." She let out a deep sigh, sounding decidedly unimpressed.

Steven wasn't surprised. It had only taken him an entire minute just to get his *name* out.

"Have a look around or whatever it is that you're supposed to do." She peered over Joe's and Steven's shoulders at the sidewalk behind them.

"What is it?" Joe asked eagerly, turning around.

"Is there a weed I should kill?" Steven wanted to know.

"Well, *no*," Karen said. "It's just . . . you *do* have your own stuff, don't you?"

"Our own . . . stuff," Steven murmured. *What stuff is she talking about?*

"We moved here from Palm Springs, you know?" Karen said with a lilt to her voice. "And we definitely didn't do any of our own lawn care there. It's unheard of, basically."

"Oh, sure," Steven said with a nervous laugh. "Of course you wouldn't." *What is she getting at, anyway?*

Joe nudged Steven with his foot. "The mower," he mumbled. "We forgot the mower."

Steven felt his jaw drop open. They'd run out of the house so fast, they hadn't even thought about bringing the mower. And now he was standing here, looking like a complete fool. What were they going to cut the grass with—a pair of scissors? "Oh, the mower! You mean, where's our *mower*."

"Well, *yeah*. It would kind of help, don't you think?" Karen leaned against the doorjamb and sighed.

"Ha ha ha ha," Steven laughed. "Of course we have our own mowing and cutting equipment. The finest available, actually. Strictly top of the line. But our usual *procedure* is to check out the . . . the *grounds* first, and do a—a—"

"An evaluation of your lawn care needs," Joe quickly added.

"Yes, a *pre*evaluation," Steven said importantly. "We want to make sure we know what we'll be dealing with, what we'll need—"

"Yeah, whatever. Just get it all fixed up by Sunday, or my mom and dad will have a cow," Karen said, sounding bored.

"So—we'll need to be here tomorrow. Early tomorrow," Joe said. He cleared his throat. "Not the crack of dawn, of course—we wouldn't want to wake anyone up—"

"Say . . . ten o'clock?" Steven suggested, taking a step closer to Karen.

"Well, when you finish your preevaluation, you'll know what time you need to get here, won't you?" Karen asked reasonably.

Steven nodded. "True. So true." *Wow. Not only is she gorgeous, she's smart too.*

He could see it now. *Me, looking cool in my new wraparound mirror shades, mowing the lawn . . . OK, so maybe I don't have those shades yet, but I have sunglasses . . . I'll take breaks to chat with her as she lounges by the pool . . . she'll casually invite me to the party on Sunday, I'll even more casually say yes. . . .*

"Ten o'clock tomorrow, then," Steven said, gazing into her eyes. "It's a date."

"Yeah. A date with you and the lawn." She closed the door in Steven's face.

"You really think we can finish everything by dusk tomorrow?" Joe asked, strolling across the Morgans' spacious backyard a few minutes later.

"No problem," Steven said, staring at the giant house. He wondered what Karen was doing right now. Maybe looking out the window—watching him! He reached down and pulled out a tuft of grass, pretended to study it, then let the clump drift to the ground. Just in case Karen hadn't been watching, he decided to repeat the process.

"What are you doing?" Joe asked, staring at the clump of grass in Steven's fist. "Pulling out each

blade of grass individually? Dude, we'll never finish this lawn if you keep that up."

"I'm not cutting it—I'm doing our evaluation,"
Steven said authoritatively.

"What's to evaluate? The grass is long, so we'll
cut it." Joe shook his head. "I think you need
another kind of evaluation. Like, a psychological
one."

"Shhh," Steven whispered, glancing at the
house. "This is important."

"Important to . . . who?" Joe looked at the house,
then back at Steven. "And what are you looking at?"

"Nothing," Steven said defensively, tossing
more grass into the air. He checked out the windows of the house again. He couldn't see anyone,
but then, he was kind of far away.

"Oh, I get it. You think you're going to impress
that girl by looking like a real gardener or something," Joe said knowingly.

"She's not *that girl*. Her name is Karen, OK?"
Steven retorted.

"So you admit it! You *are* completely crazy. You,
impress Karen? In what decade?" Joe scoffed. "She
practically slammed the door in your face when
you said the word *date*."

"Maybe she was in a hurry, OK? Maybe she was
going somewhere," Steven argued.

"Yeah, and when she finds out you like her,
she'll probably really be in a hurry to go somewhere," Joe said with a laugh. "Dude, you're way
off base if you think she's interested in *you*."

"How can you say that? Look, she just met me," Steven said. "Once she gets to know me, it'll be different. She was playing hard to get, that's all."

"Yeah, right. Hard for *you* to get," Joe commented.

Steven frowned at him. Having a best friend like Joe wasn't exactly easy either! How dare Joe say that he couldn't get a date with Karen? It wasn't totally beyond the realm of possibility. It could happen!

"OK, then. If you're so sure I can't get a date with Karen, why don't we make a bet," Steven said, smiling at Joe. There was nothing he liked better than winning bets. "By the time we finish landscaping here tomorrow, I'll have a date with her—for tomorrow night."

"Whoa, Wakefield! You really want to make it that tough?" Joe asked. "Anyway, what's your problem? I thought you were dating Cathy Connors."

Steven bit his lip. He thought about Cathy, and how much he liked her. OK, so maybe they were officially a couple. But it wasn't like they'd agreed not to date other people. Anyway, Karen wasn't "other people" . . . she was Karen, the girl Steven had dreamed about meeting his entire life. "Cathy wouldn't mind," he told Joe. "It's just one date. And besides, she's visiting her aunt in New York this weekend."

"How convenient," Joe muttered. "So you're telling me that you're going to get a date with Karen for tomorrow night. For sure."

"I'm not worried," Steven said nonchalantly. But now that he thought about it . . . what if Karen already had plans for Saturday night? It was only one day away! *Well, she'll just have to change her plans. To include me.*

"And if you don't get this date? Then what?" Joe asked, his arms folded across his chest.

Steven tapped his foot against the ground, pretending to test the soil as he considered the bet. He wanted to pick something that would make Joe absolutely miserable. Something he'd never do. Something he could rub in for years afterward. Something that would be completely distasteful to both of them.

"I know!" Steven cried, the solution coming to him like a psychic vision. "If I win, then *you* have to fill in one night for my sisters, baby-sitting for all those Riccoli kids!"

Joe chewed his fingernail. "How many Riccoli kids are there, exactly?"

"Nine or ten at least," Steven said with a wicked smile.

"Hmmm." Joe nodded. "OK, it's a deal. But Steven—are you sure you can look after so many kids all at once?"

"*You're* the one who needs to worry about sharpening your baby-sitting skills," Steven said, feeling confident. "By the way, you *do* know how to change diapers, don't you?" He snickered. Winning this bet was going to be so much fun. He'd have a date with Karen, and Joe would have a date with—disaster!

* * *

"Now, I've told the neighbors you'll be here all weekend and asked them to check in on you from time to time, make sure you and the kids have everything you need," Mrs. Riccoli explained on Friday evening. "You know, I would have asked one of them to baby-sit, but they've all got young kids themselves and—"

"It's OK," Jessica said. "We can handle it. Right, Elizabeth?"

"Sure thing," Elizabeth agreed, giving Mrs. Riccoli a confident smile.

We'll just . . . stay off the third floor, that's all, Jessica thought, looking around the kitchen a little nervously. *And make sure nobody has any matches.*

Mrs. Riccoli glanced at the clock above the kitchen sink. "Then I'd better get to the airport pronto, if you two think you have everything under control. The kids are in bed or in their rooms—all you need to do is tuck them in again for me, and of course I'll call tomorrow to check on everyone and—"

"Mrs. Riccoli, everything's going to be fine," Jessica assured her. "You left your phone number in Florida for us, didn't you?"

"Right there." Slipping her coat over her shoulders, Mrs. Riccoli pointed at the memo board on the refrigerator. "Now, let me see . . . have I forgotten anything?"

Jessica picked up Mrs. Riccoli's suitcase. "Here you go."

Mrs. Riccoli's face turned pink. "Honestly, I don't know what I'd do without you two."

"I'll help you bring your stuff to the car," Elizabeth offered, lifting the suitcase.

"And I'll go check on the kids," Jessica said. "Tell your mom we hope she gets well soon!" She waved to Mrs. Riccoli, then ran upstairs to Nate's room. When she peeked in, Nate was standing in his crib, trying to get a look out the window.

"Hey, Nate! How are you doing?" Jessica asked brightly.

"Mommy gone," Nate complained, looking very sad.

"I know. But you know what *that* means." Jessica wiggled both her eyebrows at Nate. "The Terrific Terrible Terrifying Tummy Tickler is here!"

Nate giggled as Jessica reached over and poked him gently in the stomach. "You're Jessica, silly!"

"Sure, some of the time I am," Jessica teased. "But some of the time . . . look out! I'm the Terrific Tiny Toe Tickler too!" She scooped Nate into her arms and started tickling his feet.

"No!" he squealed, laughing. "You're Jessica!"

"You should have seen Nate when I tried to get him to sleep," Jessica said, walking into the living room. "He was so funny! He kept asking me whether I would marry him, and I said, Nate, I'm flattered, but you're kind of too young for me, and *he* said I should wait for him, and—hello? Elizabeth? Are you listening?" She walked toward her sister, who was slumped in the big easy chair by the fireplace.

Elizabeth let out a tiny snore and snuggled under the blanket.

Jessica sighed, looking at her watch. Well, that was just great. That meant she was all alone. Since when did Elizabeth fall asleep so early on Friday nights? They usually stayed up at least until ten to watch a TV movie together.

Jessica flopped down on the couch. Now what was she supposed to do? She'd finally gotten all the kids into bed and had even managed to cheer them up. They were all bummed about Mrs. Riccoli going away and their grandmother being ill. Now she had hours and hours of free time to kill. *I should be at the movies with Lila and the rest of the Unicorns!* she thought, resting her chin on the arm of the couch.

Elizabeth twitched in her sleep, muttering something. *I hope she doesn't have that horrible nightmare I had the last time we were here.* Jessica decided to keep an eye on Elizabeth, just in case. But her sister looked so peaceful, Jessica couldn't feel too concerned. Besides, watching Elizabeth sleep was making Jessica sleepy herself.

She picked up the remote control and turned on the TV, turning the volume down low so it wouldn't wake Elizabeth. Then she grabbed the red wool afghan off the back of the couch and snuggled into it.

Now this is more like it, Jessica thought, channel-surfing until she hit the movie of the week. *Hey—isn't that the same actor who plays Briggs on* The Guilty and the Glamorous? She leaned forward, perching on the edge of her seat.

Elizabeth walked up the curving stairs to the third floor. Cautiously she opened the door to the secret bedroom. *I can't believe I'm going back in here after what happened last time. What am I doing? Am I crazy?*

Elizabeth peered inside, then checked behind the door. She heaved a sigh of relief. She didn't see anything unusual. But just to be safe she took an old, dusty comic book off the bedside table and jammed it under the door, propping it open. She wasn't about to be locked in a second time.

When she straightened up, she heard a wheezing noise behind her. *That's weird,* she thought, looking all around the bedroom. *It almost sounds like someone's in here.* But that was impossible—the place had been sealed up for years. Nobody besides her and Jessica even knew about it.

It's probably just the wind, Elizabeth consoled herself. *Maybe the rainstorm Jessica was talking about earlier is finally here.*

She turned around to look out the window. Instead of seeing the window behind her, though, Elizabeth found herself looking at something small, sort of hunched over. It almost looked like a giant doll. She was about to reach out and touch the doll when the figure moved, lifting its head. Two menacing eyes looked up at her.

It's the monster! Elizabeth's heart pounded in her chest as she took a step backward, preparing to flee.

At that exact moment the door she'd so carefully propped open slammed shut with a bang.

Elizabeth backed up against the door. "N-No," she gasped. "Please, don't—"

The monster reached out with large, clawlike hands. The flesh on its face was melting, and as it stepped closer to Elizabeth she saw the monster's eyes were glowing, as if a fire burned within.

"What—what do you want?" Elizabeth stammered.

The monster didn't answer. Instead it reached out, its arms oozing, and wrapped its claw fingers around Elizabeth's neck!

"No!" she screamed, gasping for air.

Six

"Elizabeth! Wake up!" Jessica shook her sister's shoulders violently.

Elizabeth sat up suddenly. Her face was pale, and her jaw was clenched tightly.

"Elizabeth, you look like you just saw a ghost or something," Jessica commented, shaking her sister's arm. "Come on, snap out of it."

Elizabeth sat up in the chair and curled her legs up underneath her. "I think . . . I did see a ghost," she said breathlessly.

"What are you talking about?" Jessica asked, perching on the edge of the giant easy chair. "Did you have a nightmare? Because I've never heard you scream like that in my entire life!" She glanced at the ceiling. "I can't believe you didn't wake up the kids."

"Jessica, it wasn't just any nightmare," Elizabeth

said. "It was that dream. The one you told me you had. The one with . . . the monster."

A picture of the monster's rotting face flashed through Jessica's mind, and she shuddered.

"I dreamed I was in the secret bedroom, and the monster—" Elizabeth broke off, clutching Jessica's arm. "Jessica, she was even worse than you said. And she trapped me inside the bedroom!"

"Did she hurt you?" Jessica asked. When she had woken up from her nightmare, her sleeve had been torn. And when Juliana Riccoli was having the nightmares about the monster a little while ago, she'd come back from a dream with deep scratches on her back.

"I don't know. She . . . the monster . . . was trying to strangle me." Elizabeth reached up and touched her neck. "I went into the secret bedroom, and I propped the door open—you know, so I wouldn't get stuck, like we did the other night."

Jessica nodded, but she was having trouble focusing on what Elizabeth was saying. She was staring in horror at her twin's neck. On Elizabeth's skin were long red marks. Ten red marks.

"What?" Elizabeth asked, sitting up. "Jessica, you look like you're about to pass out!"

Jessica forced herself to breathe normally. "There are marks on your neck!" she said. "Finger marks, Elizabeth."

Elizabeth gasped and touched her neck. "I don't . . . how could—"

"It doesn't make sense," Jessica broke in. "I mean,

I was sitting right here the *whole* time you were asleep. So how did some monster strangle you!"

"I don't know. . . ." Elizabeth said slowly. "And I don't think I want to know. Jessica, we're here for the whole weekend. What's going to happen next?"

"What happens next is that you and I have to stay *awake*," Jessica declared firmly. She didn't know how, but she wasn't about to drift into some nightmare—and end up strangled!

"I'll get it," Jessica said when the telephone rang about ten minutes later.

"Thanks," Elizabeth said from her curled-up position on the couch. "I don't think I could talk to anyone right now."

It's probably Todd, Jessica thought as she picked up the phone on the third ring. He was supposed to come over and help them that night. "Hello?" she answered.

"Hi, Jessica," Mrs. Wakefield greeted her. "How are you guys doing over there?"

"Oh, Mom." Jessica sighed, relieved to hear her mother's voice.

"What? What is it? You sound so worried!" her mother said. "Is everything OK?"

No, Jessica thought. *In fact, everything's very, very weird.* But she couldn't exactly tell her mother what had just happened. When she even thought about describing her and Elizabeth's nightmares out loud, they seemed ridiculous. Besides, her mother was acting really bizarre and stressed out lately—

Jessica sort of felt like she had to protect her.

"Sure, Mom—everything's fine," Jessica said nervously. "Uh, what's up with you?"

"I just wanted to make sure you two were doing all right," Mrs. Wakefield said. "I hate to think of you guys alone in that big house."

Jessica laughed uneasily. "We're not alone, Mom. There are five kids sleeping upstairs!"

"You're sure that everything's all right, then?" Mrs. Wakefield asked.

"Don't worry, Mom. We'll be fine!" Jessica told her as confidently as she could.

Alice Wakefield set the phone back onto its cradle on the wall. Jessica had sounded awfully calm. *Well, why shouldn't she be?* Alice thought. There probably wasn't anything to worry about—not anymore. Not as there was when she used to babysit at the house. Especially back during that time, that October . . .

Alice quietly closed the door to Eva's bedroom. The little girl had awoken with a nightmare, and Alice had sat by her bedside, singing lullabies until Eva had fallen asleep again.

Alice tiptoed down the old, creaky staircase and went into the kitchen, flicking on the light over the table. Sitting down, she pulled her math textbook from the stack of books on the table. Then she picked up a pencil and a sheet of notebook paper and started figuring out the first problem.

All of a sudden there was a strange noise. The sound of someone—or something—scratching on the window.

Alice slid back her chair. What was that? *she wondered, trying not to be afraid. A cat, maybe?*

Then she heard another noise, as if somebody were walking around upstairs. She stood up and went to the kitchen doorway. "E-Eva?" she called softly. Maybe the little girl just wanted a drink of water.

But there was no reply from upstairs.

Alice looked around the kitchen, wondering if the sound could have been made by a mouse or the Sullivans' new kitten. She peered under the stove and refrigerator but didn't see anything.

Just as she was about to return to her homework, she heard another scratch at the window over the kitchen door. Taking a deep breath, she parted the curtains and looked out.

She sucked in her breath. Three figures were standing on the stoop—looking right at her!

"Are you going to let us in or what?" one of them asked, laughing.

As Alice's eyes adjusted to the dark night, she could just barely make out their features. It wasn't three strangers—it was three of her friends! Dyan Robbins, Walter Egbert—and Jim Wilkins. Alice felt herself flush. She had liked Jim for a long time. She was even hoping they might go out on a date sometime soon. She smiled and opened the door wide. "Hey, you guys! What are you doing here?"

Jim strode into the kitchen. "We thought you could use some company."

Alice bit her lip. She would like some company, but Mr. and Mrs. Sullivan didn't want her to have guests. "I could, definitely, but—"

"Yeah, I bet. If I were you, I'd be bored to tears. Sobbing, actually." *Walter Egbert grinned, stepping through the door into the kitchen. "Baby-sitting, ugh."*

"Hi, Alice!" *Dyan Robbins came into the kitchen, carrying a quart container of ice cream. "We brought a treat. All we need are four spoons."*

Alice couldn't help grinning. It was such a relief to have her friends around after her rough night with Eva. And she supposed that a short visit wouldn't hurt. "You guys have to be really, really quiet," Alice whispered, opening the silverware drawer. "Eva's asleep."

"OK," *Jim whispered back, grinning at her. "We definitely don't want to wake her up."*

"Yeah," *Walter agreed in a soft tone. "Because once we do, then we'll have to baby-sit too."*

Alice hit him playfully on the arm with one of the spoons. "Anyway, Alice," Dyan said, setting the carton of ice cream on the counter, "we came by because we wanted to make sure we're all going to hang out on Halloween together. You're still planning to come to the school party, right?"

"Of course," *Alice said. "I wouldn't miss it. But did you guys really have to come by tonight to ask me? I mean, you could have just called."*

"Wait. I think I'm hurt," *Walter said, tapping his chin with a spoon.*

"We came to invite you in person because . . . because . . ." *Dyan looked at Jim for help.*

"Because this is a big night, and the plan's important." Jim smiled at her. "I wanted to make sure we could spend it together. I mean, all of us," he quickly added, blushing.

"Right. Of course," Walter teased him.

"Anyway," Jim went on, "what's your costume going to be?"

Alice wiggled her eyebrows mischievously. "I told you before—it's a secret. You'll find out on Halloween."

"No fair!" Walter cried.

"Shhh," Alice reminded him. She took a big bite of ice cream and glanced at the clock over the sink. "Uh-oh. The Sullivans are going to be home in a few minutes. You guys have to leave."

"But we just got here," Jim protested.

"I know—but Mr. and Mrs. Sullivan don't want me to have guests while I'm baby-sitting," Alice said. "Thanks for coming over, though. And thanks for the ice cream!" She took a final spoonful as her friends prepared to leave.

"Well, don't forget about our Halloween plans," Jim said as he opened the back door. "I can't wait to see your costume, whatever it is."

Alice grinned. "It'll be fun, I promise!"

She waved her spoon at them as they headed outside.

All of a sudden Jim turned around and came back into the kitchen. He took the ice cream container off the counter. "Don't want to leave any evidence that'll get you in trouble," he said.

"Thanks," Alice told him. "Good thinking."

Jim hovered in the doorway for a moment. He cleared

his throat. "Hey, Alice? Maybe after the Halloween party at school . . . we could go out for some ice cream or a pizza or whatever together." He shifted uncomfortably. "Just, you know. The two of us."

"Oh—definitely," Alice said shyly. "That sounds like fun." She couldn't believe it—she and Jim had a real date planned!

"Well, good night, I guess." Jim headed out the door, closing it softly behind him.

Alice leaned against the door, watching him run to catch up to Dyan and Walter. Jim was so nice! He always thought of everything. We're going to have a great time together on Halloween! *she thought happily.*

"No offense, Jessica, but this movie is really boring," Elizabeth grumbled.

"What? How can you say that?" Jessica replied. "Are you even looking at Briggs?"

"Who?" Elizabeth stared at the screen. Had she missed something? "Who's Briggs?"

"Look, if you have to ask, just forget it," Jessica snapped. "He's only the star."

"Oh, that guy." Elizabeth shrugged. "He's all right, I guess. But I thought his name was Tony. How come you call him Briggs?"

"If you watched the hottest soap on TV, you'd know. Now be quiet," Jessica warned her. "I don't want to miss this part." She leaned forward, staring at the TV. "He's going to tell her his secret password!"

Elizabeth raised one eyebrow. *Big deal,* she

thought. For some reason she couldn't get that excited about a computer mystery movie—at least, not this one. The mystery at the Riccolis' house seemed much more interesting . . . even though the memory of her nightmare an hour earlier still gave her goose bumps. Somehow she couldn't stop thinking about it. . . .

How can a dream . . . leave marks on your skin? she wondered. It didn't make any sense. It wasn't even in the realm of logic.

But if it wasn't a dream . . . could a real monster have scratched her?

That's silly, Elizabeth, she told herself. *No monster lives upstairs on the third floor. Nobody's coming to get you. Don't be so paranoid!*

But if that *wasn't* true, then why was she having the nightmare? And how did the marks on her neck get there if a real monster wasn't upstairs?

Elizabeth was so frustrated, she flung a couch pillow to the floor. "None of this makes any sense!"

Jessica turned to her. "Elizabeth, I've explained this plot like a hundred times already. See, that guy wants—"

"Not the movie," Elizabeth said, frowning. "That dream I had. And the dream you had. And how we ended up with scratch marks and torn clothes!"

Jessica's face fell. "Did you have to remind me? I was finally starting to forget about all that."

"I'm sorry. But I'm afraid that if we don't

figure it out . . . we're going to be in even more danger," Elizabeth told her. She mulled over the evidence again. Maybe there was some weird place that existed . . . a state of mind between being awake and being truly asleep. And when she got to that place, if the monster showed up . . . maybe she'd have enough strength to resist it . . . her . . . whatever! Maybe she could find out something that would help them to once and for all get rid of the monster that seemed to haunt the Riccolis' house.

"Jessica, I have an idea, and I need your help," Elizabeth finally announced.

"OK, sure. What is it?" Jessica asked, sounding a little bored.

"I'm going to fall asleep on purpose," Elizabeth said, picking up the couch pillow and patting it as she prepared to lie down.

Jessica stared at her, openmouthed. "Are you out of your mind?"

Elizabeth shook her head. "Listen. I want you to watch the clock—on the VCR there's a clock." She pointed to it. "Keep your eyes glued to that. And when I've been asleep for five minutes, you have to wake me up. You absolutely have to, OK?"

Jessica frowned. "I don't get it."

"I don't either," Elizabeth confessed. "But maybe this time, since I won't be in a deep sleep, I can find out something about what's going on."

"Are you sure you want to do this?" Jessica asked, looking concerned.

Elizabeth shrugged. "What other choice do we have? We can't stay awake all night."

"Well, I can," Jessica declared. "There's a movie marathon starting at nine. But go ahead, try whatever you want if you think it'll help."

"Five minutes, remember?" Elizabeth urged, snuggling under a blanket.

Jessica nodded. "Five minutes."

Seven

"*Sub*titles?" Jessica exclaimed. "They didn't say it was a *French* movie marathon."

She glanced at the clock on the VCR. Elizabeth had taken a while to fall asleep, but she'd finally drifted off at a minute or two before nine o'clock. *I'll wake her up at 9:03,* Jessica told herself.

She pressed the remote, skipping past channels with boxing matches, home-shopping deals, and old black-and-white sitcoms. *Isn't there anything decent on?* she wondered. It was Friday night, after all. Weren't people supposed to relax and have fun on the weekends?

She paused at a nature program, where the photographer was tracking a leopard family in the African desert. It wasn't really Jessica's favorite kind of show—there was no drama, no romance. Not between people, anyway. The only sound was of exotic, chirping insects and dry grass rustling.

Jessica stared at the leopards roaming around, waiting for something to happen. Would they leap out at the passing hyena? Would they guard their young? Would they get anything to eat in the next week?

She watched as the leopard cubs flopped down, tired from playing so much. The mother leopard licked them slowly, cleaning their fur until they fell asleep, rolling over on their backs.

Jessica rested her head on the arm of the couch. They were so cute! She blinked a few times, trying to stay awake. The photographer turned up the microphone on his video camera, amplifying the sound of the leopards' slow, sleepy, purring breathing.

Jessica had never heard a more peaceful sound in her entire life.

Elizabeth stood at the bottom of the stairs, looking up to the third floor.

That's funny, she thought, touching an antique gold-framed mirror in the hallway. *I don't remember seeing this on the wall.*

She stared at an unfamiliar, blurred painting of flowers in a field. That didn't seem like Mrs. Riccoli's style at all, Elizabeth thought. Glancing down at her feet, she noticed the carpeting was gone too. Highly polished wood floors shone in the overhead light.

Without wanting to, Elizabeth felt herself putting her hand on the banister. She climbed to the third floor. She was heading straight for the secret bedroom again. *But I don't want to go back,* she thought. *Isn't Jessica supposed to be waking me up right about now?* Still, her feet took each step firmly and deliberately, as if in protest.

When she reached the top of the stairs and looked down the hall, Elizabeth gasped. The secret bedroom she and Jessica had discovered wasn't secret anymore! The door wasn't hidden or locked . . . and as she stood in the bedroom doorway Elizabeth noticed that the windows weren't boarded up with wide, heavy slats of wood. Even the glass door out to the balcony and widow's walk was visible—not just visible, but wide open!

A cold, damp breeze blew into the room. Elizabeth wrapped her arms around her shoulders. *Jessica, where are you?* she wondered. *Wake me up already!* She walked over to the balcony door and was about to close it when she heard a voice behind her.

"I've been waiting for you," the voice said.

Elizabeth's spine tingled. *OK. Here's your chance,* she told herself. She slowly turned around, expecting to see the monster. But nobody was there.

"Over here, silly," the monster cackled in a gravelly voice.

Elizabeth turned again—and again—and again—spinning around until she came face-to-face with the monster.

"Found me!" it said with an evil laugh.

Elizabeth jumped back, bumping into a bookshelf. A few books toppled onto the floor with a crash. "Stay away from me!" she cried. *Come on, Jessica!*

Wake me up—now! "L-Leave me alone!" she sputtered at the monster.

"Never," she growled, reaching for Elizabeth's
neck with strong, scary fingers.

"What do you want from me?" Elizabeth wailed,
squirming out of its reach.

The monster picked up an old, scarred teddy
bear from the bed and pushed it at Elizabeth. "You
are going to pay," the monster threatened. "You . . ."
A look of sadness and disgust crossed the monster's
distorted face. Then suddenly it lunged at Elizabeth,
putting its hands on her throat.

"J-Jessica!" Elizabeth screamed, half choked.
"Jessica, wake me up!" She thrashed about, just
barely managing to slip out of the monster's grasp.

She turned, trying to dart for the door. But
somebody was standing there, blocking her way.

"Jessica!" Elizabeth wailed. "What are *you* doing
up here?"

"That's what I want to know," the monster
growled, moving toward both of them.

Elizabeth grabbed her sister's arm. Before Jessica
could say a word, Elizabeth yanked her toward the
bedroom closet. She pushed Jessica inside and went
in after her, closing the door firmly behind her.

"Hold the door as tight as you can," Elizabeth
told her.

Jessica stared at Elizabeth, her face completely
pale. For the first time Elizabeth could remember,
her twin didn't have anything to say. She nodded
and pulled tightly on the doorknob.

For a brief, terrifying moment everything was completely silent. Elizabeth could hear nothing but the pounding of her own heart. Beside her Jessica bit her lip as she strained to hold the door closed.

Maybe we'll be OK, Elizabeth thought. *Maybe the monster's given up on us.*

Jessica took a deep breath, looking up at Elizabeth with frightened eyes. Elizabeth was about to tell her she thought they might be out of danger when she heard something strange. As if someone else were in the closet with them, breathing.

That's impossible, she told herself. *The monster must be standing outside, waiting for us.*

"You can wait as long as you want!" Elizabeth called out boldly. "We're not coming out!"

"Good," the monster replied, its breath hot on Elizabeth's ear. She turned sideways, her eyes widening. The monster was in the closet with them! But when—how? "That will make everything so much easier," it wheezed, putting one hand on the front of Elizabeth's neck and starting to squeeze.

"Jessica! R-Run!" Elizabeth gulped.

But she was too late. Dropping the old teddy bear to the floor, the monster wrapped its other hand around Jessica's neck!

We're both going to die! Elizabeth realized, pushing at the monster with her last ounce of strength.

No ugly monster's going to kill my sister! Jessica began kicking the creature. "Let her go! Let me—"

Jessica blinked. Where was that bright light

coming from all of a sudden? Had someone opened the closet door?

When she could finally focus, she discovered that she wasn't fighting any monster. She was looking right into the eyes of Todd Wilkins!

"What's the deal?" he asked. "You guys practically tried to kill me when I came in! I mean, I know I'm *late,* but—"

"Elizabeth!" Jessica sat bolt upright on the couch, pushing aside a tangle of blankets. "Were you just dreaming what I was dreaming—about being stuck in the closet with the monster?"

Elizabeth had sprung to her feet. "I thought we were going to die!"

Todd laughed. "Watching too many scary movies again?" He glanced at the TV. "What's on, anyway?"

"Speaking of movies," Elizabeth said, frowning at Jessica. "You were supposed to wake me up after five minutes—not fall asleep watching some old movie marathon!"

"I didn't fall asleep watching any movie marathon," Jessica protested, folding her arms across her stomach.

"Then how do you explain what just happened?" Elizabeth demanded.

Jessica shrugged. "For your information, I was watching a show about the geography and social habits of leopards."

Todd turned around and stared at her. "Now I *know* you were dreaming."

"I don't care what you were watching," Elizabeth broke in. "The point is, you promised you'd save me." She shuddered. "And instead you came into my dream, and the monster had us in the closet—"

"Whoa." Todd held up his hands. "Time out. Would somebody please explain what you're talking about?"

"I don't know," Todd said after Jessica and Elizabeth had spent fifteen minutes detailing their dream, as well as the other weird happenings at the Riccoli house that he hadn't heard about yet. "Are you sure it's . . . as real as all that?" he asked.

"Todd, is this real enough for you?" Jessica pointed to the scratch marks on Elizabeth's neck.

"And look at that," Elizabeth said, touching the torn sleeve of Jessica's T-shirt. "She definitely didn't have that rip when we got here."

"Yeah, but if you guys were both asleep . . . you could have both dreamed about having a fight . . . and like fought each other," Todd suggested. "I mean, you *were* both on the couch. . . ."

Jessica held out her hands to Todd. "Does it look like I have fingernails long enough to make scratches like that on Elizabeth's neck? My fingernails are about as dull as—as yours," she told him. Staring at her nails for a second, Jessica felt chagrined. They really looked awful. She hadn't been in on a Unicorn manicure in a long time. "Anyway, I definitely wouldn't go around scratching Elizabeth's neck, asleep or not!"

"Well, no," Todd said, "probably not. But—"

"And you were here with me when Juliana had all those nightmares," Elizabeth reminded him. "Remember how she kept saying that someone—a monster girl, she said—was trying to get her in her dreams and how afraid she was?"

"Sure, but . . . nothing happened," Todd argued.

"Except that she ended up with big scratch marks too!" Jessica told him.

"OK, but she's not having those nightmares any-more," Todd said, sounding triumphant. "So! How do you explain *that*?"

"Well, duh!" Jessica cried, rolling her eyes. "She's not having them anymore because the monster's more interested in getting *us*! Isn't that much obvious?"

Todd looked almost hurt. Jessica was a little sorry she'd had to be so blunt, but really. Todd wasn't usually such a blockhead about things.

"What Jessica *means* is . . . we know our story's hard to believe," Elizabeth said. "I mean, who wants to believe this stuff? But it happened, Todd." She rubbed her neck. "You have to trust us."

"Hm," Todd grunted.

"Look, Elizabeth, if Todd doesn't want to know the truth, there's nothing we can do. He'll just have to find out for himself," Jessica declared, throwing off the afghan and standing up to go into the kitchen for a drink of water.

"J-Jessica? What's that?" Elizabeth pointed to something brown and furry that had fallen off Jessica's lap onto the floor.

Jessica shrugged. How was she supposed to know what it was? It looked like a stuffed animal of some kind—probably belonging to one of the kids.

Todd picked it up and turned it over, examining it. "I thought you guys were a little old for teddy bears. But on second thought, this teddy bear looks a little old for *you*." He handed the teddy bear to Jessica.

As soon as she felt the bear in her hand Jessica recognized it. This wasn't just any old teddy bear. "Oh, my gosh," she breathed.

Elizabeth nodded, her face pale. "The monster was holding a teddy bear. An old, ratty one. Is—is that it?"

Jessica looked at a tag sewn onto the stuffed bear's arm. "This bear belongs to Eva Sullivan," she read out loud.

"Who's Eva Sullivan?" Todd wondered.

"She used to live here," Jessica said, her heart beating faster. "In this bedroom upstairs—the one that was all boarded up. The one that we dream about going to. And I don't know what happened to her, but . . . I have this weird feeling that she's . . . the one."

"The one?" Elizabeth repeated. "You mean . . . the monster?"

Jessica swallowed hard, setting the teddy bear on the floor. "The monster must be Eva Sullivan."

Eight

◇

"I'm sorry, Elizabeth, but none of this makes sense," Todd said. "Bringing a teddy bear back from a dream? Come on." He stretched out on the living room floor. "You guys are trying to play some kind of practical joke on me. But it's not going to work, so you can forget about it."

Jessica sighed, discarding an eight of clubs. "All I can say is, I've warned you. Don't fall asleep."

"Jessica's right," Elizabeth chimed in, picking up the eight and discarding a three. She and Jessica were on their fourth game of gin rummy.

Elizabeth looked at her watch. The way things were going, they'd probably have to play a *hundred* and four games to make it through the night. "You really shouldn't sleep—not in this house," she told Todd.

"Yeah, well, thanks for the warning, but . . ."

Todd yawned. His eyes were already closed. "I played basketball for three hours this afternoon."

"Is that our fault?" Jessica replied.

Elizabeth frowned at her. "Todd didn't know he'd have to stay up all night."

"Well, neither did we," Jessica said. "Not really, or I never would have told Mrs. Riccoli we'd baby-sit while she went to Florida. I mean, if I were her, I'd come back, get all my kids, and *move* to Florida. Not that I've ever been there, but I'm sure it's a nice place to live, especially when you buy a house that's not haunted by some creepy old monster named Eva." She picked up a card from the deck, then laid another on the discard pile. "Gin."

Just after Elizabeth started to count the points in her hand, she heard a snore. Todd had drifted off to sleep while Jessica was talking!

"We'll have to keep an eye on him," Elizabeth said, watching Todd, whose face was buried in a pillow.

"Let's use the five-minute rule," Jessica suggested.

"Yeah, only let's stick to it this time, OK?" Elizabeth said, shuffling the cards for their next game. "No dozing off."

"Look, I *said* I was sorry! How many times do I have to apologize?" Jessica complained.

"I just don't want anything to happen to Todd, OK? I didn't mean to rub it in," Elizabeth said, even though she still felt angry at Jessica for letting her down. If Todd hadn't shown up when he did, they might not have come back from the dream.

Elizabeth hadn't figured out much from her so-called experiment, but she did know that weird place between being awake and being asleep existed. And she also knew that she never wanted to visit it again.

"You know what?" Jessica said, turning around in her chair to look at Todd. "Todd's out. Like, completely. And he's totally fine. So what *I* think is . . . maybe this Eva Sullivan only wants to hurt *girls*!" Her face lit up as if she were pleased with having come up with the theory. Then she frowned. "Not that that's good news for us."

Elizabeth considered it for a moment. "Well, it started with Juliana, and then there's us . . . wait. What about the fire in Andrew's room when he was asleep?"

Jessica shrugged. "We still don't know how that started. I mean, Andrew could have done it."

"Yeah, but he probably didn't," Elizabeth said. "And if this Eva monster person wants to get *all* of us, setting fire to the house was the perfect setup." She watched Todd sleeping. He really did look very relaxed, like nothing could bother him.

But suddenly his legs jerked back and forth, as if he were trying to run. Elizabeth stiffened. "Jess, how long has it been?" "I don't know. Five or six minutes, I guess," Jessica said. She turned around and looked at Todd. "Why?"

Before Elizabeth could say anything, Todd began thrashing, throwing off the blanket and straining to get away. "No!" he yelled. "Stop!"

Elizabeth and Jessica jumped out of their chairs and rushed to his side. Elizabeth shook Todd's arms while Jessica patted his face. "Todd, wake up!" Elizabeth urged.

"Todd!" Jessica screamed.

Todd's eyes popped open, and he stared up at Elizabeth, a terrified expression on his face. "She . . . she's horrible," were the first words out of his mouth.

Elizabeth sank onto the floor beside him. "I know."

"So much for my girls-only theory," Jessica moaned.

"Good morning, everyone!" Amy said brightly as she and Winston walked into the Riccoli kitchen on Saturday morning.

Jessica turned around from the sink and glared at her. "What's good about it?" she muttered.

"Gee, looks like somebody's not a morning person," Amy remarked with a smirk.

Actually, Jessica thought, the one very good thing about morning was the fact that it was actually *here*. It meant that she, Elizabeth, and Todd had made it through the night—without falling asleep once. Now they'd get to take off for several hours while Amy and Winston baby-sat the kids. Jessica couldn't wait to go home and get into bed.

"And how are my favorite little troublemakers today?" Winston asked, setting a large duffel bag filled with various sports equipment on the floor.

"You twouble," Nate said with a giggle. "Not me!"

"OK, well, we'll see about *that*." Winston reached over and tickled Nate's stocking feet.

"Did you bring your volleyball net again?" Andrew asked, jumping out of his chair. He poked through the bag until he found the short, kid-size net. "Awesome!"

Jessica went over to the table to grab some more dishes to wash. She hated washing dishes with a passion. But she figured that the sooner she finished, the sooner she could go home.

"Are you all done?" Jessica asked Juliana, lifting her plate off the table.

Juliana nodded. "I love pancakes! Can we have them again tomorrow?" she asked, looking up at Jessica.

"Sure! Whatever you want!" Jessica offered, smiling at her. "That is, whatever *Todd* feels like making." She gave him a superior look.

"Yay!" Juliana cheered. "I'm going upstairs to get my doll, OK?" She practically leaped out of her chair and charged out of the kitchen.

At least some people around here got a good night's sleep, Jessica thought.

"I'm going out to play," Andrew announced.

"Me too!" Gretchen cried. "I can beat you at volleyball, you know."

"Can not," Andrew replied.

"Can too!" Gretchen said.

"Sounds like you guys need a referee," Winston said. "Wait one second and I'll go with you. Jess, any more pancakes over there on the griddle?"

"Dream on," Jessica muttered. "What do I look like, your personal chef?"

Winston looked taken aback. "Somebody didn't get up on the right side of the bed this morning."

"More like some people didn't get up at all," Jessica corrected him. "Because they didn't go to sleep."

"So how was last night?" Amy asked, sitting down at the breakfast table next to Elizabeth, who was busy helping Nate finish his apple juice.

"We'll tell you about it later," Elizabeth muttered wearily.

"You guys look like you haven't slept at all," Amy commented.

Jessica nodded. "Exactly."

Amy looked confused. "What—were the kids up all night? Did they miss Mrs. Riccoli?"

"You can explain," Jessica told her twin. "But as soon as I finish washing those plates, we're *out* of here."

Steven polished off his second glass of orange juice and set the glass in the sink. He couldn't wait to get over to Karen's house and start mowing the lawn. Of course, he wasn't exactly looking forward to the *mowing*—he was just psyched to impress Karen with his wit and personality.

"Don't forget—we're having that big dinner party tonight," his father told him. "So you might want to make some other plans."

"No problem," Steven said, feeling confident.

He was going to make other plans, all right—he'd
be going out with Karen!

Steven caught a glimpse of his reflection in the
kitchen window and felt the smallest twinge of
doubt in his stomach. Not that he looked bad or
anything. But did he look good *enough*? If he lost
his bet with Joe . . . he'd be heading over to the
Riccolis' with Jessica and Elizabeth. *Ugh. Don't
think about it.*

Mr. Wakefield set down his coffee cup. "Now,
are you sure you guys have thought of everything
you'll need for the job today? The weed cutter?
Clipping and pruning shears? Extra gasoline?"

"Dad!" Steven sighed. "Do you want to come
with us or something?"

Mr. Wakefield looked embarrassed. "Sorry. I was
just thinking that maybe Mr. Morgan has a lot of
rich friends. If you and Joe do a good job, this
could lead to more work."

*Why do I get the feeling this is leading into some-
thing like my allowance being cut off?* Steven thought.
Anyway, impressing Mr. Morgan was the last thing
on his mind. Impressing *Karen* was what mattered.

Steven ran upstairs to his bedroom and closed
the door, checking his reflection in the full-length
mirror on the back of it.

He took off his plain gray T-shirt and put on his
new white sleeveless "muscle" T-shirt. The shirt
showed off his tan arms. He was no weight lifter,
but he had *some* definition in his biceps. If he
clenched his fists, anyway. And he looked cool in

his favorite long, baggy, official L.A. Lakers shorts.

Who wouldn't want to go out with me? He slipped his sunglasses out of his pocket and put them on. He turned to the left, checking his profile. Then he turned to his right. He crouched over, pretending he was riding the mower. *I think my right side is better. I'll have to make sure that's the side she sees when I go by her house,* Steven thought, imagining Karen watching him. Then he faced the mirror, grinning as he pictured Karen opening the front door. He waved. "Hi there," he said, winking at the mirror.

Suddenly the door swung open.

"Wakefield, what are you doing?" Joe pointed to Steven's sunglasses.

"Getting dressed, what else?" Steven replied quickly.

"What, is the light too bright for you?" Joe asked with a smirk.

Steven stiffened and adjusted the sunglasses on his face. "I, uh, just didn't want to forget them, that's all," Steven said.

"Well, here's something else I hope you didn't forget." Joe handed Steven a sheet of paper with "The Bet" scribbled in giant letters at the top. "If you don't mind signing that, then we can get going."

"Sign it? What are you, a lawyer?" Steven laughed, skimming the paper quickly. It outlined their basic agreement, including the punishment for losing the bet: baby-sitting at the Riccolis'. "Sure, I'll sign it," Steven said, grabbing a pen off his desk. He scribbled his signature and was about to hand it back to Joe when a panicked thought struck him: getting a date with *anyone* for a Saturday night at the last minute was practically impossible. Even when it was someone he dated a lot, like Cathy Connors. Was he making a big mistake?

He glanced over his shoulder at his reflection in the mirror again. *Nah.*

Steven handed Joe the signed bet, then walked over to the door. "Let's get going."

"Yeah, you're going to need all the time you can get," Joe teased, stuffing the sheet of paper into his back pocket. "Not to mention . . . shoes?" He pointed at Steven's bare feet.

"I was getting to that." Steven reached under his bed and rummaged around until he found his favorite leather basketball sneakers, the coolest pair he owned. He shoved his bare feet into them and turned to Joe. "So. What are *you* doing tonight? You're going to be all alone, aren't you? Isn't that sad. Oh, right!" He smacked himself on the forehead. "You won't be alone—you'll be surrounded by all those little kids, screaming at you, asking for bedtime stories—"

Joe grinned. "We'll see, Wakefield." He patted his back pocket. "We'll see."

"Honey, you look like you haven't slept at all!" Mrs. Wakefield said, opening the kitchen door to let in Elizabeth. Jessica was right behind her. "Same goes for you!"

That's because we didn't sleep at all! Elizabeth thought, putting her backpack on the counter. "Yeah, we're a little tired," she confessed.

"My daughters the zombies," Mr. Wakefield said, setting his newspaper on the table. "Taking care of five kids is a little more than you bargained for, I bet."

"I'll say." Jessica headed for the stairs. "I'll be sleeping. Wake me up in time for dinner."

"What? No shopping today? But—it's Saturday!" her father teased.

"Dad, please. I'm really not in the mood for jokes," Jessica told him. She dropped her duffel bag on the floor and practically crawled up the stairs.

Mr. Wakefield raised his eyebrows at Elizabeth. "What's with her?" he asked Elizabeth, putting down the newspaper and standing up.

"You know Jessica," Elizabeth said with a shrug. "She needs at least ten hours of sleep a night or she gets grumpy."

Mr. Wakefield laughed. "That's true."

"Anyway," Elizabeth continued. "Now that Amy and Winston are taking the day shift, we can sleep and get rested up for tonight."

"Sounds like a very demanding job," Mr. Wakefield commented. Elizabeth looked at him and smiled faintly. "You have no idea."

Elizabeth sat down at the kitchen table about ten minutes later, slumping over in her chair. She was completely drained. But before she went upstairs and climbed into her bed, she wanted to ask her mother a few questions. Especially now that her father had left for the grocery store and the two of them were alone.

"Mom? What do you know about Eva Sullivan?" Elizabeth asked, looking up at her mother, who was buttering a piece of toast.

Mrs. Wakefield gave a start. She dropped the knife and it clattered onto the table. She cleared her throat and gave a nervous laugh. "Oh, how clumsy of me. I've been dropping things all morning!"

Elizabeth smiled wanly. She wasn't letting her mother off the hook so easily. "So?" she pressed.

"So . . . well, I feel like a klutz," Mrs. Wakefield said, brushing a lock of hair back from her forehead. "And I've got all those people coming over tonight and—"

"No—about Eva Sullivan," Elizabeth broke in. "Who was she?"

Alice Wakefield set down the knife. "Why are you asking about her?" She sounded agitated.

"Um, well, because," Elizabeth said, a bit put off by her mother's tone. Why was she so set against discussing Eva Sullivan? "Well, we know that she lived at the Riccoli house. And we found this . . . thing that belonged to her, with her name on it. I don't know."

Elizabeth wasn't sure how much she should tell her mother. Whenever she mentioned the Sullivans, her mother seemed to clam up and get nervous. And then there was the time Jessica had brought her to the house to help Mrs. Riccoli with some interior decorating. Mrs. Wakefield had suddenly, on the spot, decided she couldn't help Mrs. Riccoli—and she'd run out of the house without explaining why.

"I've told you guys a dozen times before," Mrs. Wakefield insisted. "I don't know anything about that . . . about her."

"But you have to," Elizabeth said. "I mean, you lived in Sweet Valley back then, right? So who was she? And what happened to her? Was it something horrible or—"

"Look, Elizabeth, I really don't have time for this," her mother interrupted, pushing back her chair. "I've got a million things to do to get ready for our party tonight. Right now I need to get to the florist." She grabbed her purse off the counter and strode out the door.

Why is she acting so weird? Elizabeth wondered. *If she does know something terrible about Eva Sullivan . . . why won't she tell me?*

Nine

Backing out the driveway in the family's new mini-van, Alice Wakefield took a deep breath to calm herself. She kept trying to forget about Eva Sullivan, and Jessica and Elizabeth kept trying to remind her! Why couldn't they leave well enough alone? Why did they want to know so much? If they kept pressing her for information, she was going to break down and tell them the truth.

But the truth wasn't easy to think about. Alice had forced it out of her mind for years. Only now it kept coming back, bit by bit. . . .

Alice had just barely gotten all her friends out of the Sullivans' house that night when she heard the front door being unlocked by a key. She rinsed all the ice cream spoons quickly and dumped them into the dishwasher, hoping the Sullivans wouldn't notice.

Alice knew she should never do something that Mr. and Mrs. Sullivan wouldn't approve of. And she did respect their rules. She swore to herself that she'd never let her friends in while she baby-sat again.

Alice hurried into the front entryway. "Hi, Mr. and Mrs. Sullivan. Did you have a good time?"

Mr. Sullivan slipped out of his coat and hung it in the closet by the front door. "Well, considering it was a bunch of boring business executives giving speeches . . . we had a great time."

Alice smiled. "Not too much fun, huh?"

"The food was excellent at least," *Mrs. Sullivan said with a rueful smile. She hung up her coat.*

"That's good. Well, I should probably get going," *Alice said.*

"Yes—what am I thinking? I'll need to give you a ride home." *Mr. Sullivan took his coat back out of the closet.*

Mrs. Sullivan followed Alice into the kitchen. Alice started packing up her book bag, shoving her unfinished math homework back into a notebook. I'll have to do that as soon as I get home! *she told herself.*

"Alice? I have a tremendous favor to ask," *Mrs. Sullivan said, sitting at the kitchen table, where Alice was gathering her things.*

"Sure. What is it?" *Alice asked, glancing at her.*

Mrs. Sullivan shifted uneasily in her chair. "I really do hate to ask you this. I'm sure you have plans already. But I honestly can't think of anyone else to ask." *She paused, looking hopefully at Alice.* "It's Halloween night. We have to go out to another company event."

"Oh." Alice made a face. "Halloween night? Who plans a company event on Halloween?"

Mrs. Sullivan rolled her eyes. "Tell me about it! There are plenty of us who'd rather stay home with our kids. But the president has some idea about having a big costume party for all Jim's clients, and so . . . we're obligated to go, really. And we were hoping you'd be available to baby-sit Eva."

Alice bit her lip. She wanted to help Mrs. Sullivan. But there was no way she could miss Halloween! She'd put so much work into her costume . . . and she was really looking forward to hanging out with her friends . . . and to seeing Jim later. "I'm sorry, Mrs. Sullivan. I do already have plans. And . . . they're kind of important to me."

"I know it's last minute," Mrs. Sullivan said. "And I know baby-sitting on Halloween's the last thing you want to do—"

"Don't get me wrong," Alice said quickly. "I mean, I love Eva. It's just . . . that night . . . it won't work."

Mrs. Sullivan drummed her fingernails against the table. "I suppose I could always pretend to be ill and skip the company party," she mused. "But since Jim's new to the firm, these kinds of events are sort of important. . . ."

"Well—what if you got someone else? I could ask around at school, or maybe you have some friends who know of someone," Alice suggested. "It's not like I'm the only baby-sitter in Sweet Valley!" She laughed.

"No," Mrs. Sullivan said slowly. "But you are the only one so far who can make Eva feel better after her horrible nightmares. And I'm sorry to say, until she stops having them, that's a bit of a requirement." She sighed. "Look, I'm sorry, Alice—this isn't your problem. I'm honestly not trying to ruin your Halloween plans! I'll figure something out."

"OK." Alice finished putting all her school stuff into her book bag. She put on her faded denim jacket and slung the bag over her shoulder. She was about to walk out of the kitchen, but she couldn't get a picture out of her mind. A picture of poor little Eva. What if she had a nightmare? What if she woke up like she had that night . . . crying, miserable . . . and what if the baby-sitter the Sullivans hired couldn't comfort Eva and make her feel better? And Halloween was the night Eva feared most of all.

Of course, Alice knew that Eva wasn't her responsibility. She was the Sullivans' responsibility. But they were really in a jam. If she could help . . .

She turned to face Mrs. Sullivan. "What time do you think you'd be home from your party?"

"I'm not sure," Mrs. Sullivan said, shrugging. "Nine or ten, I'd guess. Why?"

"Well, maybe I could baby-sit for part of the night," Alice offered. "If you could be home kind of early—I could go out afterward and meet my friends. I'd miss the school party, but—"

·"Oh, Alice! Would you?" Mrs. Sullivan cried, jumping up from the chair and throwing her arms around her.

Alice blushed. "Sure. But you guys will come home as soon as you can, right?" she asked Mrs. Sullivan, turning around as she opened the front door.

Mrs. Sullivan nodded. "We'll only stay as long as we have to."

"Great! Then I can have two Halloween parties. One with my friends and one with Eva." Alice smiled. Maybe everything would work out after all.

Steven wiped the sweat off his forehead with the back of his hand. Then he pushed his sunglasses up the bridge of his nose. They kept slipping off, which was interfering with his plan. *I look like a nerd, pushing my glasses up all the time. Why don't I just clip a pocket protector to my T-shirt too?*

Not that Karen was watching. Steven stole a glance at her. She was sitting in a chair by the pool, reading a magazine. And she was looking just as gorgeous as she had the day before, in a bright pink one-piece bathing suit, her blond hair fanning over her shoulders.

But so far Steven hadn't managed to do anything but *look* at her—he hadn't said word one to her yet. Steven checked his watch. It was already twelve-thirty. If he didn't get moving, he didn't stand a chance of landing a date with her tonight.

Just then Karen looked up from her magazine, her gaze traveling across the lawn to Steven. He gulped. This was his big moment—the one he'd been waiting for!

He revved the engine and lunged forward, executing a quick turn that tipped the mower slightly to one side. Then he charged down the lawn in the other direction. Out of the corner of his eye he snuck a look over at Karen.

She was holding the magazine directly in front of her face.

Steven took his foot off the accelerator, coasting to a stop. This wasn't working out at all! *Time to try another tactic*, he told himself. But there were only so many tactics when you were on a mower, he quickly realized. He could mow . . . or he could mow. At least he didn't have the incredibly boring job of trimming all the edges. That was Joe's problem.

Steven grinned, heading diagonally across the front lawn, then made another cross . . . then went in a circle. After a while, he couldn't tell which part he'd cut and which he hadn't. Just to be sure, he went back over a couple of sections.

"Wakefield!" Joe called. "Hey, Steven!" He waved his arms from the front step.

Steven cut the motor. He looked over at Karen and smiled. She was staring right at him. *Yes! Finally she notices!* he thought, smiling back at her. "Yeah?" he called to Joe, trying to sound gruff. "What is it?"

"What are you *doing*?" Joe demanded. "Are you *trying* to make weird patterns in the grass?"

"What do you mean?" Steven replied, glancing around him. "It looks . . . it looks . . ." *Like one of those strange crop circles they keep finding in England's farm fields—the ones no one can explain.*

"Yeah, what is *up* with that?" Karen asked, standing to get a better look. "Are you trying to send a message to an airplane?"

"Maybe it's an SOS!" Joe laughed while Karen

put her hand over her mouth to cover a giggle.

Steven's heart sank. Sometimes attention wasn't a good thing. *Thanks a lot, Joe!* he thought angrily.

Elizabeth sleepily sat up in bed, stretching her arms over her head. She had only been asleep for a few hours, but she felt a hundred percent better. Back in the quiet safety of her own bedroom, it was hard to believe what had happened at the Riccolis' house the night before. But she knew it had happened, and that it was real. As much as her mother denied it, something horrible had happened to Eva Sullivan—or else that girl-monster haunting them didn't make any sense. Not that *any* of it made any sense as far as Elizabeth was concerned.

She lay back down and closed her eyes. She was going to need a lot more sleep if she wanted to stay up all night again. Elizabeth punched the pillow a few times and rolled over, trying to get more comfortable.

But as hard as she tried, she just didn't feel like sleeping. It was the middle of the day. And even though Elizabeth had a lot of unanswered questions, there was one thing she knew for sure: it was Saturday! The one day of the week that she didn't have to do anything. No writing for the school newspaper, no homework—nothing!

She threw off the covers and climbed out of bed. Then she went down the hall and peeked in at Jessica, wondering if she felt the same way—tired, but not sleepy. "Jess?" she whispered, pausing in the doorway.

Her sister didn't answer. She didn't even budge. The blanket was pulled over her head, as if she were trying to shut out the entire world.

Elizabeth grinned. She should have known. Jessica was a master sleeper.

Elizabeth went back to her room and grabbed her robe. On her way to the shower she stopped to call Maria. Maybe they could go for a bike ride together or hang out at the beach. *I have to do something normal and fun or I'll go crazy!* Elizabeth thought.

What? Steven took off his sunglasses and rubbed his eyes. Was he seeing things? Was that Joe, lounging by the pool with Karen? Not lounging, technically—but cutting the grass around Karen's chair so that he was only about two feet away?

That figures, he thought angrily. Of course Joe wasn't going to play fair. No, he was taking every opportunity to angle in on *his* date. Joe knew how Steven felt about Karen—he should be keeping his distance!

Steven charged over on the mower toward the pool. He ran over a large stick, sending it flying through the air. Then he swerved to avoid a rock and bumped over a giant exposed tree root, nearly tipping over. He barely managed to come to a stop at the edge of the patio surrounding the pool.

"Wow. That thing can go pretty fast, can't it?"

Karen observed lazily from her lounge chair.

"You should see it on the highway," Joe told her, his eyes flashing.

Karen laughed. "It goes from zero to fifty-five miles an hour in—"

"A couple of hours, tops," Joe filled in, making her laugh even harder.

Steven wasn't amused. "Joe," he said coldly, shutting off the mower's engine. "I need your help with something."

"Well, I'm kind of busy over here," Joe protested, busily cutting the grass right around Karen's chair.

"I can see that you are," Steven said through clenched teeth. "However, I need your, ah . . . input on a delicate . . . mowing matter."

"You guys really take this stuff seriously." Karen got to her feet, shaking her head. "Chill already. It's only a lawn." She strode across the patio and disappeared into the house.

"Nice going. You've got her totally charmed," Joe teased.

Steven glared at him. "Well, I *would* if you weren't sitting over here, pretending to clip grass and hogging all her attention for yourself!"

"Hey." Joe shrugged. "You *told* me to trim the edges. I'm trimming them."

"Well—can't you trim them somewhere else?" Steven demanded, getting off the mower.

"Not until you mow some more, no," Joe replied. "Of course, it's taking a little longer than usual since you're driving in circles, but—"

"Oh, so now you have a problem with my mowing technique?" Steven demanded, stepping in front of Joe.

"Technique? Is that what you call it?" Joe scoffed. "I thought you were just trying to make this job last as long as possible by having to go over every single area twice."

"It's called being thorough," Steven said defensively, poking Joe's chest.

"It's called being sloppy," Joe retorted, stepping closer so that they were staring right into each other's eyes. Joe opened and closed the clipping shears right at Steven's knee.

I could always run him over with the mower, Steven thought for a fleeting second, glaring at his best friend. He'd never felt so competitive in his entire life. "If I'm sloppy, then you're downright—"

"Lunch!" Karen called cheerfully, flinging open the sliding door and walking out with a tray of sandwiches.

Ten

"So what do you call these? They look delicious!" Steven said, taking a crustless sandwich off the tray on the table. *What's wrong with crusts, anyway?* he wondered. The sandwiches were so tiny, he was going to have to eat twenty of them. He peered at the filling, which was a strange greenish color.

"They're cream cheese and olive," Karen told him. "Mother's favorite. Don't ask me why. She thinks they're low calorie or something, which is so not true." She shook her head.

"Anyway, it's not like *you* need to worry about calories," Joe said, scooting his chair closer to Karen's.

Steven felt his stomach turn over. He wasn't sure whether it was the weird sandwich he'd just eaten in one bite or Joe's annoying attempt to flatter Karen. Wasn't that *his* job? "So, Karen. What's *your* favorite kind of sandwich?" Steven asked, moving his own chair closer to Karen. She was surrounded now.

"Hmmm." Karen thought it over for a second while Steven struggled to chew and swallow. Spitting out the sandwich would definitely *not* make a good impression. "Veggies and cheese, I guess," she said. "I hardly eat any meat."

"Really!" Steven cried. "Neither do I. Actually, for a while I was a pretty serious vegetarian." Of course, "a while" meant a week or two, but Karen didn't need to know that.

"You're kidding. Really?" Karen asked, looking at Steven with surprise. It wasn't the nicest look Steven had ever gotten, but at least she had noticed he was alive and sitting at the table with her.

"Oh, yeah. I got into it pretty seriously," Steven said. "I did a lot of studying and reading about it— you know, how much energy is wasted producing red meat—"

"I know—isn't it incredible?" Karen was gazing at Steven with what looked like respect.

Now if I can just get her to go from respect to love . . . I'll be set! Steven searched his mind desperately for some other information he could haul out to impress her with. "Oh, yeah. And the way they treat chickens. I mean, I'm telling you, I didn't eat meat for—"

"At least a week," Joe interrupted. "And then one day he just cracked. He ran down to this burger place by the beach and got the one pounder. Didn't you?" He laughed.

"A burger?" Karen repeated. The look of respect slowly vanished, like a deflating balloon.

Steven felt the blood drain from his face. "Well, the doctor said I needed iron," he said quickly. "Getting anemic and all." He glared at Joe. There was no question now that Joe was deliberately trying to ruin any chance he had with Karen. But he wasn't going to let it happen. Once Karen saw the real Steven, she'd like him—he was sure of that. He sipped from his glass of iced tea and decided to change the subject. "So, are you going to be attending Sweet Valley High with us?"

"I suppose." Karen sighed. "Daddy went on and on about some horrible-sounding private school nearby, but I told him, I simply cannot wear a uniform every day." She flicked her hair over her shoulder. "A person has to be able to express her individuality somehow, don't you think?"

"Oh . . . definitely," Steven agreed. *And you can express it to me . . . whenever you want!*

"Dress codes are so uncool," Joe said. "Anyway, Sweet Valley High's a good school—we've got some great teachers and lots of good sports teams, and the parties aren't bad either. If you want any help picking your classes—"

Steven kicked Joe under the table, cutting him off midsentence.

"Hmmm," Karen muttered, looking slightly worried about something. She made a face and put down her sandwich without eating a bite.

"Sorry," Joe said with a laugh. "Didn't mean to

bring up classes. I guess I ruined your appetite."

"That's kind of how I feel about school!" Steven joked. "I mean, uh . . ." He felt flustered, wondering how to interpret the look of disgust on Karen's face. Did she like classes? Hate them? Did she study? Was she a slacker? How was he supposed to impress her when he didn't know anything about her?

"Hey," he said, sitting up. "I have an idea. I could take you for a tour of the school." He was just about to say, "Maybe tonight!" when Karen pushed her chair back from the table and stood up.

"Do you guys smell something?" she asked, wrinkling her nose and looking around.

"What? Is it the mower? Gosh, I shouldn't have parked so close—the clippings smell is probably ruining your appetite. I'm sorry!" Steven got to his feet. "I'll move it right away."

"No, it's not that," Karen said slowly. "It's almost like . . . you know when something gets left out in the rain for too long? And afterward it gets this rotten, musky smell, like a dead animal?" She sounded breathless and dramatic—almost as if she were delivering a line in a play.

Joe looked at Steven, raising one eyebrow. "I don't smell that. But—maybe we did something to the lawn. Maybe you ran over—"

Steven shook his head. "I didn't."

"You know what it is? It's like . . . a late autumn night, and your shoes are wet, covered with leaves because you walked home in the rain, alone,"

Karen said, pacing around the patio. "And you forget to take them off right away because you had this poem you wanted to write, but there they are and—"

Steven glanced at his feet and the sneakers he'd pulled out from underneath his bed. *No. It can't be,* he told himself. Just when he was starting to make progress!

They were the same sneakers he'd been wearing last week when he jumped off the mower into the pool on a hot afternoon, without thinking. Because they were leather, they'd never quite looked—or smelled—the same since. To make matters worse, Steven wasn't even wearing any socks!

"Yeah, I . . . uh . . . think I know what you mean," Steven said with a nervous smile at Karen. "You know, what you were just saying about, uh . . . leaves and all . . . it reminded me of something we forgot back at my house. We need some . . . bags. You know, to put all the . . . leaves in," he stammered.

Joe looked at him, confused. "Bags?"

"I don't see any leaves," Karen commented.

"Be right back!" Steven cried, dashing across the lawn. *Why didn't I just say, "Hi, my feet stink—will you go out with me?"*

Jessica lay in bed, staring at the ceiling. She wasn't getting up until she absolutely had to. She was due back at the Riccolis' at five o'clock. From five o'clock until . . . the sun came up on Sunday morning.

And she'd have to stay awake the entire time.

Wait a second! Maybe I don't have to! Maybe I could ask Mom and Dad to let us have all the kids stay over here tonight! she thought, feeling a surge of excitement. Juliana could stay in Jessica's room, they could put Nate's crib in the den . . . kick Steven out of his room and give it to Andrew instead . . . it could work!

Then Jessica remembered that her parents were having a big dinner party that night for several of their friends and even some business associates. They'd never go for the idea. Jessica sighed, rolling over in bed. There was nothing to do but stay up all night. She forced herself to get out of bed and then trudged down the hallway to Elizabeth's room.

Elizabeth was lying on her bed, reading a book. "Hi, sleepyhead," she greeted Jessica, moving over so that Jessica could lie down beside her.

"How come you're all wide awake and dressed and everything?" Jessica mumbled.

"I couldn't sleep more than a couple of hours," Elizabeth said. "I guess it was the daylight or something. Anyway, I went for a bike ride with Maria, and—"

"Elizabeth, are you crazy?" Jessica gave her sister a gentle shove. "You're going to be so tired tonight!"

"No, I won't be," Elizabeth protested. "I mean, I'm so wound up about everything, I think I'll be up for days. I can't even focus on this mystery!" She dropped the book onto the floor.

"Well . . . just make sure you *stay* wound up," Jessica warned her. "Hey, did you talk to Amy and Winston?"

Elizabeth nodded. "I explained what happened last night. At first they didn't believe me, but when Todd told them the same story, they called back to say we're *all* staying at the Riccolis' tonight. That way we'll be safe."

"Oh, good." Jessica sighed and rolled over. "Though I can't really imagine Winston saving me from a spider, never mind a creepy monster who wants to kill me."

Elizabeth laughed. "Who knows, maybe Winston will surprise you."

Jessica smiled. "I guess he could always fend her off with some really bad jokes."

Steven turned onto Larkspur Way and ran toward the Morgans' driveway at top speed. Of course, having his running sneakers on helped. His new, fresh nylon running sneakers that didn't stink—at least not yet.

Stupid, smelly leather sneakers. I'm never buying any again! He'd thrown his old ones into the trash as soon as he got home.

Steven turned into the Morgans' long driveway and started jogging up toward the house.

Hey! What's this? Steven thought, his heart hammering in his chest as he saw Karen standing on the front steps to her house. She was waving at him—and smiling!

Steven started running even faster. *She missed me!* he thought happily. *She's realized how amazingly hot and charming I am, and she can't wait to see me again!*

He waved at Karen as he headed up the long driveway. He was vaguely aware that a car was coming up behind him. Glancing over his shoulder, he saw a black four-wheel-drive Jeep. *Probably Mr. Morgan,* he thought, *coming back from his three rounds of golf.*

Steven sprinted faster, keeping pace with the Jeep. The Jeep moved slightly ahead, and Steven pumped his legs and arms, trying to outrun it. *I'll show Karen what an awesome athlete I am. Then she'll never be able to turn me down.*

The Jeep shot past him and pulled up to the doorstep with a screech of the brakes. "Jake! I thought you'd never get here!" Karen called. She hopped into the Jeep and closed the door, and the Jeep took off around the circular driveway.

Steven stood beside the driveway, panting, and stared inside as the Jeep passed by. Karen had her arms around the driver—a tall blond guy who looked like he was in college. Steven coughed a few times, breathing in clouds of the Jeep's exhaust.

Joe looked over the top of a hedge that lined the driveway, grinning from ear to ear. "So. How much exactly does baby-sitting pay these days, anyway?"

Eleven

Elizabeth shut off the overhead light in Olivia's room. "You can read for a while if you want," she told the oldest Riccoli girl. "But don't stay up too late, OK?"

"I won't," Olivia said, propping her back against the headboard. "Elizabeth?"

"Yeah?" Elizabeth stopped in the doorway.

"Thanks a lot. For staying here while Mom's gone, I mean," Olivia said. She smiled. "It's nice to have someone we know around."

Elizabeth managed to smile back. "We like being here!"

Well . . . not exactly, she thought as she gently closed the door and walked around the second floor, checking on the other kids. Everyone besides Olivia had drifted off to sleep about an hour ago.

Elizabeth stood in the doorway to Juliana's

room for a second, gazing at the little girl's sleeping figure. Juliana looked safe, as if she weren't having scary nightmares anymore. Elizabeth was relieved. She hated hearing Juliana cry or seeing her so upset.

Elizabeth went back downstairs to the living room, where the rest of the baby-sitters were sitting in a circle on the floor. Music videos were playing on TV.

"Did you guys realize that we have the perfect ratio going? We have exactly one kid per baby-sitter," Amy said. "That should be enough to deal with any problems that come up, right?" She laughed nervously.

Elizabeth sat next to her. "Sure. Any problems with the kids, we can handle. But anything else . . ."

"Look, we've agreed," Todd declared. "We know how we're going to handle it."

Elizabeth couldn't help noticing that nobody wanted to say exactly what "it" was. It was almost as if they thought just mentioning the word *monster* or *Eva* would be enough to summon her.

"Yeah," Jessica added. "We're going to sit here like this all night, and nobody's going to close their eyes."

Winston groaned, rubbing his back. "I don't know if I can sit here *all* night. I might have to sit on the couch at some point. Here—anyone want a cookie? My mom came by this afternoon to drop these off. Not that she'd even come in the house for some weird reason—"

"You're kidding!" Jessica exclaimed. "Your mom too?"

"What do you mean?" Winston replied.

Elizabeth propped her elbows on the floor and rested her chin in her hands. "Our mom is acting so weird about us baby-sitting here! I mean, you know how calm and rational our mom is. But now it's like she losing it or something. First she barely even came into the house to meet Mrs. Riccoli," Elizabeth said. "And then this morning, when I asked her about Eva Sullivan, she practically ran out of the house—after insisting she didn't know anything and telling me to quit bugging her!"

"Wow," Amy breathed. "That doesn't sound like your mom at all."

"And remember how happy she was yesterday, when we told her we were quitting?" Elizabeth turned to Jessica. "She totally encouraged us. Is anyone else's parents acting weird about us being here baby-sitting?"

"Oh, yeah. Definitely. I mean, I hardly said anything when I went home this morning. I just mumbled about how I didn't get a good night's sleep," Todd said. "Then I asked my parents if they knew anything about the family that used to live there."

"And what did they say?" Elizabeth asked.

"They acted like they'd never even *heard* of the Sullivans," Todd said. "Then they told me to go to bed, like they wanted to drop the subject as fast as they could."

"When I told my mother I was going to work

here, she got all pale and weird looking," Amy said. "She said she just wasn't feeling well all of a sudden, like she had the flu or something. But whenever I mention coming here, it's like she doesn't want to hear anything about it—at all."

"They all must know something," Todd guessed. "So why won't they tell us what it is?"

"Yeah," Jessica added. "It's not like they're protecting us. I mean, if they really wanted to protect us or thought something was wrong—wouldn't *they* be here instead of us?"

"Well, when my mom was here to drop off the cookies," Winston began, "I tried to tell her about us having to stay awake all night because a monster might get us in our dreams. She looked at me like I was crazy."

"So what else is new?" Jessica teased him.

Winston raised one eyebrow. "The fact that you're not spending your Saturday night with the Unicorns, gossiping about me?"

"Please. The Unicorn Club has much more interesting things to talk about," Jessica declared.

"Sure they do," Todd teased. "Like the price of lipstick."

"Ha ha," Jessica said. "I don't *wear* lipstick, OK? It's called lip *gloss*."

"Oh. Well. Excuse me!" Todd said, laughing.

"So . . . what do you guys want to *do*?" Jessica asked everyone about fifteen minutes later. "We have an entire night to kill." She laughed nervously, realizing what she'd just said. "I mean, to use up."

"Yeah, try ten hours or so," Todd complained.

Jessica sighed. "I already looked at the TV schedule for tonight, and it's incredibly lousy. If only there was something decent on TV, like *The Guilty and the Glamorous*," she said. "If only I could *be* on *The Guilty and the Glamorous*, going out with Briggs to talk about my new modeling career, at a coffee-house for a late night cappuccino—" Suddenly Jessica snapped her fingers. "Hey, that's it!"

"That's it? As in, that's it, you've finally and completely lost your *mind*?" Todd asked, staring at her.

Elizabeth laughed. Jessica already sounded as if she were delirious from lack of sleep and it was still early!

"No, that's it—cappuccino! That's what we need!" Jessica declared.

Elizabeth raised an eyebrow. "Jessica, we don't drink coffee. And we definitely don't know how to make cappuccino."

"Please!" Jessica exclaimed. "How hard can it be?" She got up and disappeared into the kitchen.

Jessica flipped through the cookbook Mrs. Riccoli had left open on the counter. "Cakes, chutneys, cookies . . . where's the section on coffee?" she asked out loud.

She grabbed a few more cookbooks out of the cabinet and looked through them too. Sure, there were recipes for drinks made with coffee, coffee ice

cream, coffee cake . . . but not for plain old *coffee*. Apparently everyone was already supposed to know how to make coffee. *Why? It's not like they teach us at school!* Jessica thought, staring at the coffeemaker on the counter in frustration.

She walked over to the coffeemaker and opened the various compartments. Something went in the top, something went in the middle, and something went on the bottom. She pondered this for a second, trying to remember her parents' coffeemaker at home. It wasn't the same kind, exactly, but the basic principle had to be the same. Pot on bottom, water on top. Coffee in the middle.

Jessica nodded, satisfied. Now all she needed was coffee grounds. She opened the refrigerator and poked around until she found a coffee can. "Aha!" she cried, prying off the top.

Her stomach turned. Instead of coffee, the can was filled with leftover spaghetti. Left over from . . . quite a while ago.

She dumped the old spaghetti into the trash disposal and went back to the fridge. In the freezer she found a can of coffee. Consulting the directions on the side, she measured several teaspoonsful of coffee into the middle compartment.

Then she filled the carafe with water, poured the water into the top compartment, replaced the carafe beneath the coffee, and flicked the switch.

"Jess? You need any help?" Amy walked into the kitchen.

"No, thanks!" Jessica said confidently, flipping

her hair over her shoulder as she watched the water begin to drip through. "It was a cinch, actually."

Elizabeth stirred milk and sugar into the steaming cup of coffee in front of her on the kitchen table. She'd never had coffee before. She wasn't sure she wanted to try it. But Jessica said it would help her stay awake, and she was feeling like she could use a boost.

Well, here goes nothing, she thought, lifting the cup to her lips.

"I feel so sophisticated," Winston said, curving his pinky finger as he picked up his own cup of coffee.

Elizabeth took a tiny sip of the hot liquid. She gagged. It tasted awful! She felt something clumpy and granular stick in her throat. "How did you make this stuff, Jessica?" she gasped.

Winston put his cup back on the table. "I did feel sophisticated. But now I feel *ill.*"

Amy smiled wanly. "I guess it's one of those tastes you're supposed to get used to."

"Jessica? It's called a filter. Look into it," Todd said, making a face.

"Filter?" Jessica asked, setting down her cup and peering into the murky depths. "What's that?"

Todd sighed loudly. "You're supposed to put the coffee grounds in a filter—that way they don't all pour through into the coffee!"

"Well, how was I supposed to know that?" Jessica asked defensively.

"Gee, I don't know. Common *sense*, maybe?" Todd suggested.

"Excuse me, but I didn't see anyone else volunteering to make coffee," Jessica said. "If you're such an expert, why don't you brew the next pot!"

"Actually," Winston said, examining the can on the counter. "There wouldn't really be much point."

Elizabeth stared at him. She'd managed to get down most of the coffee in her cup. She'd swallowed it as though it were cough syrup, pinching her nose shut so she couldn't smell it. "There wouldn't be any point? Why not?"

"Because it's decaffeinated," Winston announced. "Which means it has no caffeine, which means it won't help us stay up. My parents drink decaf after dinner so that they can go to *sleep*. Which means we drank this horrendous stuff for no reason at all!" He glared at Jessica.

"Well, sheesh." Jessica set the coffeepot in the sink. Her friends had been attacking her about her little coffee blunder for what seemed like an hour. "I had an idea. I tried to help. And all I get in return is a bunch of criticism. I suppose you guys are so smart, you know some perfect solution to staying up all night that I just haven't thought of. So go ahead. Tell me what it is." She dumped her coffee cup in the sink and turned to face everyone, arms folded across her chest.

"Well . . . we could listen to the radio," Amy suggested. "Really loud. And we could dance and—"

Elizabeth pointed to the ceiling. "We'd wake up all the kids. We can't do that."

"Hmpf!" Jessica snorted triumphantly. *It isn't so easy, is it?* she thought.

"Well . . . how about if we make a bunch of prank phone calls!" Winston suggested excitedly. "You know, bug a bunch of people we know and—"

"We can't tie up the phone line like that," Amy said, shaking her head. "What if Mr. or Mrs. Riccoli tries to call us?"

"Uh-huh." Jessica nodded. "Right again!"

"I know!" Todd said. "Let's play some board games. Whatever the Riccolis have—we'll play them all. We can call it . . . the Riccoli Olympics! Whoever wins the most games will be this weekend's champion!"

"Sounds good," Elizabeth told him.

Board games? All night? Jessica sighed. "Well, I *guess* it'd work." She hated to admit that Todd had come up with an even halfway decent idea.

"Fine with me," Amy said with a shrug.

They all followed Todd into the living room, and he opened the tall wood cabinet in the corner where Mrs. Riccoli kept the kids' board games.

"I have to warn you all . . . I'm a master of board games," Winston said. "An absolute master. Especially chess, checkers, backgammon—"

Todd reached into the cabinet and pulled out a stack of games. "Let's see. To make it fair, someone else close their eyes and pick the first one we'll play. You can pick, Elizabeth."

Elizabeth closed her eyes and reached out, trying to grasp one of the games balanced in Todd's arms. "This one!" she said, pulling one out of the stack.

"Candy Land it is," Winston said excitedly. "Of course, not *quite* as challenging as chess, but I can adapt."

"It says on the box that this game is for kids age two to *six*," Todd complained.

"Then you'll probably do really well!" Jessica told him, laughing. "But don't count on it."

Steven stood back on the Morgans' lawn, staring around at his master work: all the shrubs, hedges, and grass he'd gone over with a fine-tooth comb. He could barely make out anything now that it was completely dark—but the final results looked pretty good, considering they'd finished by moonlight.

"I can't believe it took us so long," he said to Joe. "We missed out on a whole Saturday night!"

"Like you had any better plans," Joe commented, picking up the clipping and cutting tools from the lawn.

"Like you did," Steven retorted, stuffing the check Mrs. Morgan had given to him into his shorts pocket.

"I guess your date with Karen will have to wait until next Saturday night," Joe teased.

"Actually that will work out perfectly," Steven said. *All I have to do is figure out how to ask her . . .*

especially now that it seems she kind of has a boyfriend.
He was just climbing back onto the mower when
headlights appeared at the end of the driveway.
The car looked familiar. *Too familiar,* he thought,
frowning as the Jeep pulled up in front of the
house.

"Good night, Jake! I had a great time! You're the
best dancer in the world!" Karen called cheerfully,
stepping down from the Jeep. "Bye!"

The guy in the Jeep honked twice, then took off,
charging down the driveway, the Jeep's motor
revving at high speed.

How obnoxious, Steven thought, glaring at the
car as its taillights disappeared down the street.
*Some people need to draw so much attention to them-
selves, it's ridiculous!*

He turned on the mower, smiling at Karen as he
loudly revved the engine. "So, we'll—I'll—see you
at school on Monday?" he said, forging ahead as
though her dissing him all day hadn't cut his ego in
half . . . or was it thirds?

"I guess so," she said. "I mean, if you're there,
and I'm there . . . we're bound to, right?"

"We'll run into each other," Steven said. *She
wants to see me again—she just said so!* Maybe the
situation wasn't hopeless after all. "Of course. Hey,
maybe we'll even be in the same classes or something. And then I was wondering, you know.
Maybe next weekend—"

"Oh, you'll have to talk to Daddy about that,"
Karen said breezily.

Talk about strict parents! Steven thought. "You mean, I have to ask his permission—"

"Sure. I mean, he's the one who decides *when* the lawn needs trimming." Karen turned to Joe. "But I'll definitely see you next Friday night— seven o'clock, right?"

"Cool." Joe beamed. "Sounds perfect."

"Let me get this straight," Steven said to Joe once Karen had gone in the house. "I have to baby-sit for the Riccolis . . . and you get to go out with Karen? Are you serious?"

"Don't take it so hard," Joe consoled him. "You know what they say. Love is blind and all that."

"Yeah, I'll say!" Steven cried. "You didn't even notice her—I did!"

"Dude, who wouldn't notice her? She's beautiful," Joe said. "Besides, you have a girlfriend—I don't!"

"But—you didn't even like her!" Steven practically shouted.

Joe shrugged, beginning to walk down the driveway. "What can I say? After you made me clip all that grass by the pool, well, we kind of got to be, you know, close."

On the mower Steven chugged slowly beside Joe. "Kind of got to be *close*? That's the lamest thing I've ever heard."

"Well, it happened," Joe said. "You know how it is. You spend a little time with someone, you start talking . . ."

Steven narrowed his eyes. A very *interesting* idea was forming in his head. "Oh, sure. I do know how it is," he replied, a small smile curving up the corners of his mouth. "Actually I got to be friends with someone today too."

"Really?" Joe replied, sounding bored. "What, were you talking to the squirrels?"

"No," Steven said slowly. "Actually Mrs. Morgan and I had quite a little chat while you were washing your hands a few minutes ago. That's why she made the check out to *me*." Stopping the mower, he pulled the check out of his back pocket and shoved it in Joe's face. "Steven Wakefield. See that?"

"Then we'll just have to go back and ask her to rewrite it to both of us!" Joe tried to snatch the check out of Steven's hand.

"Ah! Not so fast." Steven lifted the check into the air, out of his reach, and started moving forward on the mower. "Have a great time with Karen next weekend. Who knows, maybe you *can* get a veggies and cheese sandwich for seventy-five cents!" He burst out laughing. Then, holding the check above his head like a victory flag, he pressed the accelerator and took off at top speed, roaring out of the driveway and onto the street.

"Wakefield! I'll get you for this!" Joe shouted.

Steven turned around to get a good look at Joe. He was struggling to run after the mower, carrying all their tools. One of the clippers banged into his shin, and Joe cried out in pain.

Steven laughed out loud. "Sure you will!" he called

back. "Maybe you'll catch up to me—tomorrow!"

All of a sudden, as he turned left at the intersection, Steven heard a loud siren. He turned around. A police car, its lights flashing, was pulling up on the street beside him.

Me? Are they pulling me over? Steven wondered, glancing around at the deserted street. *But . . . why? I'm not even driving. Not technically, anyway.*

The car door swung open and a female police officer walked up to Steven. "Son? Can I see your license and registration, please?" the police officer asked, stopping beside the mower.

Steven coughed. "But . . . it's a *mower*."

"I can see that." She smiled.

"So . . . what's the problem?" Steven asked. "Er, officer . . . ma'am?"

"The problem is, you cannot go charging down a city street in a motor vehicle at night without lights!" the officer told him. She took a ticket book out of her back pocket. "We're looking at several violations here. Let's see . . . where should I begin? How about with your name?"

Steven shrugged, trying to look innocent. "I didn't mean to cause a problem. I was in a hurry because—"

"Name?" the officer prompted.

"See, what happened was—well, it's kind of funny, actually, depending on how you look at it." Steven laughed nervously.

"Name?" the police officer asked again, tipping the brim of her hat to get a better look at him.

Steven sighed. "Stupid. *S-t-u-p-i-d*," he spelled out for her.

The officer frowned. "Are you trying to insult an officer? That's another violation, you know."

"I was talking about me!" Steven cried. He slumped down in his seat. "Oh, what's the use." He unfolded the small piece of paper in his hand. "Will you take a check?"

Twelve

"Listen. I don't care if it is Park Place," Jessica declared. "I'm not paying five hundred dollars a night to stay there!"

Normally she thought Monopoly was a pretty good game, as far as games went. But instead of owning a lot of fancy property, she was stuck with a couple of loser railroads that nobody ever landed on. In her opinion they ought to be airports, not railroad stations—maybe then she could get more than twenty-five bucks out of people for stopping on the squares.

"Sorry, Jessica, but you know the rules," Todd told her with a grin.

"Yeah, yeah." Rolling her eyes, she handed her last five hundred bill to Todd. "All I can say is, there'd better be a Jacuzzi in my room."

Amy laughed. "You really take this game seriously, don't you?" she asked.

"Jessica likes to win," Elizabeth said in a stage whisper. "Once when we were playing with Steven, she made him go bankrupt *eight times*."

"But if he went bankrupt . . . didn't he lose the game?" Todd asked, looking confused.

"I gave him a loan," Jessica said. "But he couldn't make the payments. So I gave him another, and another . . ." She smiled. That *had* been one of her better Monopoly moments. Tonight, on the other hand, she was fighting for last place with Winston. She snuck a glance at Winston's pile of cash, trying to estimate how much he had left and who was in worse shape.

All of a sudden Winston's chin dropped, bumping his chest. He was sound asleep! "Winston!" Jessica cried.

Amy reached over and shook him. "Don't fall asleep! Winston, wake up!"

Winston jerked awake, swaying slightly. "Get out of jail free!" he cried. "Do not pass go, do not collect—"

"Winston, you fell asleep," Jessica told him, frowning. "You can't do that!"

"Oh. Well, it's just that it was such a long time since my last turn," Winston said. "I guess I drifted off when Elizabeth was building her cottages over there on Marvin Gardens. How much are those, anyway?" He eyed his playing piece, which was nearby. "Is there some other road I can take?"

Instead of handing the dice to Elizabeth, Jessica

put them down in the middle of the board. "Let's do something else. If this is making Winston tired, then we'd better move on." *Besides,* she thought, trying not to look too excited. *This way, I won't officially lose!*

Amy rubbed her stomach as she put her money back into the bank. "Does anyone else feel like they could be on a commercial for stomachache medicine?"

"It's the coffee," Elizabeth said. "I know. I feel kind of disgusting too."

Jessica sighed. She'd had more than enough of everyone complaining about her coffee idea. Was it her fault the coffee was unfiltered, stale, and decaf? Who was she supposed to be, Ms. Coffee?

She frowned. *If only I could come up with another idea. Then maybe everyone would get off my back about the stupid coffee.*

What would everyone really love? she wondered. *Probably to go to sleep right now—like Winston just did. Luckily for him we were all here to watch him and wake him up.*

Just then Jessica realized something: Winston hadn't said anything about a nightmare. *Maybe that's a good sign,* Jessica thought. He probably hadn't been asleep long enough to fall into that weird half-dreaming state. If there was only a way they could all sleep for just a few minutes, they'd stay out of danger—and they wouldn't be completely exhausted! *But how do we make sure we wake up before we fall into a deep sleep? We need some-*

thing programmed, something like—an alarm clock!

"Wait a second!" Jessica cried, jumping to her feet. "I know what we can do!"

"Drink tea instead of coffee?" Todd asked, smothering a yawn.

"No, it's way better than that," Jessica declared. "Just wait right here, and *don't* fall asleep." She ran over to the circular stairs and dashed to the second floor. Carefully she opened the door to Mrs. Riccoli's bedroom. She quietly crept to the bedside table, rummaged around for the alarm clock's cord, and unplugged it from the wall.

Then she ran back downstairs, holding the alarm clock high above her head. "Ta-da!" she cried. "This is the solution to all our problems." She plugged the cord into an outlet and put the alarm clock in the center of the Monopoly board. "Winston just had a little nap. And nothing happened to him because we were right here to wake him up before he drifted into a deep sleep. But you feel better, right, Winston? You feel refreshed, don't you?"

Winston's eyes were half shut. "Well—actually—"

"Anyway, that's not the point," Jessica went on. "The point is, all we need to do is reset this alarm for every ten minutes. That way we can all sleep—but no one will ever be asleep longer than ten minutes. Which means no one will be asleep long enough to get into trouble with—you know. Her."

Elizabeth looked at her sister intently. "That sounds like it could really work."

"Sleeping through the night ten minutes at a time? Hey, at this point I'll try anything," Winston said.

"Great idea," Amy told her. "You're awesome."

Todd just shook his head. "I *think* . . . it's the best idea you've ever had! It's brilliant, Jessica."

She shrugged, sitting back down in the circle. *Awesome. Brilliant. An angel. The compliments are really piling up lately*, she thought as she set the alarm clock.

The young girl watches as, one by one, the baby-sitters drift off to sleep. Soon they are all sleeping soundly. The tall one with brown hair snores slightly— snores, as if he is so relaxed, he feels right at home. But he isn't at home, the girl thinks. He is in my house.

Those five annoying kids in my living room are so sure they have a plan. The girl glares angrily at them. They think they're so smart. Especially that blond-haired girl who looks so much like her mother. She thinks she can outsmart me. But that isn't going to happen. Not tonight.

Every ten minutes, when the alarm sounds, they all jerk awake, looking stunned. One of them hits the snooze button, resetting the alarm, and then they all go back to sleep right away, as if nothing has happened.

Snoozing, the girl thinks with disgust. I'll show them snoozing. They can snooze until—

And then suddenly, before she can make a move to

unplug the alarm clock, one of the boys stands up, stretches his arms over his head. It's the boy she's heard make so many jokes. He smacks his lips as if he's thirsty. The girl watches as he moves toward the kitchen, taking a long stride forward with his right leg.

Snap! His foot yanks the alarm clock's cord out of the outlet on the wall.

The girl stares happily as the numbers on the clock flash red one final time, then go out.

Very good, she thinks with a wicked smile. Thank you. That's one more thing I don't have to take care of. . . .

Jessica climbed up the stairs to the third floor, once again noticing all the strange details that didn't match the Riccolis' house. Only this time she felt different being there. She felt relaxed, almost. She knew why: She didn't have to worry about what would happen next. The monster could never get her—not in a mere ten minutes. And even if she didn't wake up with the alarm clock, one of her friends would, and then Elizabeth, Amy, Winston, or Todd would come to her rescue.

So there, monster, she felt like saying but decided not to push her luck.

She stood at the top of the stairs, staring at the exposed wall where the secret bedroom had once been hidden. Now it was wide open, as if inviting her in.

But she didn't go into it. She was heading somewhere different this time . . . somewhere new. Her feet led her to a ladder in the hall—a wooden ladder that creaked and groaned beneath her weight as she climbed. Then she pushed open a hinged door in the ceiling—and stepped out onto the roof.

Jessica gasped, looking out over the edge of the giant house. She was four stories up! Nervously she rested her hand on the balcony of the widow's walk, trying to keep her balance. *What am I doing way up here?* she wondered, looking around the roof. She felt so exposed . . . so vulnerable.

A strong, cold wind was blowing against her back as she gazed out toward the ocean. Only she couldn't see the ocean. The sky was completely dark: no moon, no stars . . . even the lights that normally shone from the town of Sweet Valley were gone. What was worse, Jessica couldn't see any lights on in the houses surrounding the Riccolis'— she couldn't even see those houses. It was almost as if nothing else existed except her on that forlorn, empty roof.

Her heart constricting with fear, Jessica stepped carefully over to the trapdoor that she'd come up through. But it was locked! She couldn't get back into the house!

She walked back to the edge and looked out, her hands shaking as she grasped the wooden railing. How in the world was she supposed to get down? Nobody even knew she was up here! Everything was so quiet, it was almost as if the entire world had gone to sleep.

She heard the trapdoor slam shut and whirled around, her eyes wide with fear. *Maybe I've been asleep too long! Maybe it's the monster!* she thought, panicking.

But it wasn't the monster who emerged from the trapdoor. It was Amy. "J-Jessica?" Amy asked, straining to make out Jessica's face in the darkness.

"Amy? It's me," Jessica said, heaving a sigh of relief. The monster was nowhere in sight.

Amy reached out for Jessica's hand. "I wonder . . . I wonder why the alarm hasn't gone off yet. It's been ten minutes, hasn't it?"

"I don't know," Jessica said, jumping as the door to the roof opened again.

Todd stepped through, the door slamming shut behind him. "I think the alarm clock might be broken, you guys," he said, joining Amy and Jessica on the widow's walk.

"B-Broken?" Jessica asked. "No way! No possible way!"

"Then . . . why are we all here?" Amy replied, peering over the edge and stepping back quickly, afraid. "What's going to happen to us?"

"Look, don't panic," Todd said. "OK, maybe we fell asleep and we're dreaming, but there's still Winston and Elizabeth—"

The trapdoor flung open with a crash. Winston stepped through, walking as if he were in a daze. "I—I couldn't help it," he said. "I couldn't wake up. I never heard the alarm clock go off."

Jessica's heart was in her throat. Now all *four* of them were trapped in the dream. Their only hope of coming back alive was Elizabeth!

But of course Elizabeth will come through. I mean, it's Elizabeth! She's been saving me practically since the day we were born! Jessica told herself.

She took a deep breath to collect herself and turned to the others. "It's going to be OK. Elizabeth will save us. She'll wake us up any minute now, and we'll go back to playing dumb board games just like before, and I don't care who wins. Elizabeth won't let us down, I know it!"

Elizabeth felt like she was sleepwalking as she stumbled up the stairs to the third floor. *Jessica said I shouldn't have gone on that long bike ride. And that I should have slept more during the day. She was right.*

Elizabeth had tried as hard as she could not to fall into a deep sleep. Every ten minutes she'd woken up, stood and stretched, then punched the snooze button if no one else had. But now it seemed like a long time ago that she'd woken up. And she was stuck in a dream that felt incredibly intense . . . and completely real.

She rubbed her eyes as she started climbing the rungs of an old, worn ladder. *Where am I going? Why can't I stop?* She climbed steadily until she reached a giant metal handle on the ceiling. Curious, she reached up to touch the handle.

The ceiling cracked open, revealing a trapdoor. *This must be the way back!* Elizabeth thought happily. *This is the way out!* She stepped through and looked around, trying to get her bearings.

"Elizabeth!" she heard Jessica cry.

"Jessica?" Elizabeth stepped toward the voice, unable to see anything in the pitch-black night. "What—" As her eyes slowly adjusted to the light she found herself staring at Jessica, Todd, Amy . . . and Winston. "Oh, no," she groaned.

"You guys know what this means, don't you?" Jessica asked fearfully.

Elizabeth nodded, her heart freezing. "We're all asleep."

For a minute nobody said anything. Elizabeth couldn't move or think—she had no idea what to do next. She only knew that she was filled with an incredible feeling of doom. "How," she muttered under her breath. "How could we have let this happen? How could I? I never should have—"

"Elizabeth, it's not your fault," Jessica said. "It's her, it's all her, everything's because of—"

A rumble of thunder cracked the air, and Elizabeth jumped, her heart beating double time. She reached out and held Jessica's hand, the way they always had when they were little, squeezing it tightly.

A flash of lightning lit up the sky, and as Elizabeth watched in horror the trapdoor opened again—and the monster, Eva Sullivan, stepped through onto the roof.

"Welcome to your worst nightmare," the monster threatened in a thick, raspy voice, heading straight toward the five of them. "Welcome to your death."

"Our . . . death?" Jessica sputtered.

Elizabeth clutched Jessica's hand as tightly as she could. A violent shiver wriggled up Elizabeth's spine. This time there was no escape. . . .

The twins and their friends are trapped in their worst nightmare. . . . Will they escape their death? Find out in Sweet Valley Twins #100, IF I DIE BEFORE I WAKE, *the terrifying conclusion of* THE FRIGHTENING FOUR *miniseries.*

Bantam Books in the SWEET VALLEY TWINS series.
Ask your bookseller for the books you have missed.

SIGN UP FOR THE SWEET VALLEY HIGH® FAN CLUB!

Hey, girls! Get all the gossip on Sweet Valley High's® most popular teenagers when you join our fantastic Fan Club! As a member, you'll get all of this really cool stuff:

- Membership Card with your own personal Fan Club ID number
- A Sweet Valley High® Secret Treasure Box
- Sweet Valley High® Stationery
- Official Fan Club Pencil (for secret note writing!)
- Three Bookmarks
- A "Members Only" Door Hanger
- Two Skeins of J. & P. Coats® Embroidery Floss with flower barrette instruction leaflet
- Two editions of *The Oracle* newsletter
- Plus exclusive Sweet Valley High® product offers, special savings, contests, and much more!

Be the first to find out what Jessica & Elizabeth Wakefield are up to by joining the Sweet Valley High® Fan Club for the one-year membership fee of only $6.25 each for U.S. residents, $8.25 for Canadian residents (U.S. currency). Includes shipping & handling.

Send a check or money order (do not send cash) made payable to "Sweet Valley High® Fan Club" along with this form to:

SWEET VALLEY HIGH® FAN CLUB, BOX 3919-B, SCHAUMBURG, IL 60168-3919

NAME_____
(Please print clearly)

ADDRESS_____

CITY_____ STATE_____ ZIP_____
(Required)

AGE_____ BIRTHDAY_____ /_____ /_____

Offer good while supplies last. Allow 6-8 weeks after check clearance for delivery. Addresses without ZIP codes cannot be honored. Offer good in USA & Canada only. Void where prohibited by law.
©1993 by Francine Pascal   LCI-1383-123